PRIMORDIAL

PRIMORDIAL
AN ABSTRACTION

D. HARLAN WILSON

ANTI-OEDIPUS

FORT WAYNE, INDIANA

PRAISE FOR THE WORK OF D. HARLAN WILSON

"Provocative entertainment."
—*Booklist*

"A bludgeoning celluloid rush of language and ideas served from an action-painter's bucket of fluorescent spatter."
—Alan Moore

"New bursts of stream-of-cyberconsciousness prose."
—*Library Journal*

"Wilson writes with the crazed precision of a futuristic war machine gone rogue."
—Lavie Tidhar

"Wacky experimental fiction."
—*Publishers Weekly*

"Fast, smart, funny."
—Kim Stanley Robinson

"Pomo cybertheory never tasted so good!"
—*American Book Review*

"Utterly original."
—Barry N. Malzberg

"If reality is a crutch, Wilson has thrown it away."
—*Rain Taxi*

Primordial: An Abstraction
Copyright © 2014 by D. Harlan Wilson
ISBN: 978-0-9892391-5-8
Library of Congress Control Number: 2014906820

First Anti-Oedipal Paperback Edition, September 2014

Chapter 47 is based on the real-life experience of Dr. Bonnie Mathies, who used to work with a pathological librarian.

Cover Design by Matthew Revert
www.MatthewRevert.com

All Ages & Headliner No. 45 Fonts by Kevin Christopher
www.KCFonts.com

Anti-Oedipus Press
Fort Wayne, IN

www.Anti-OedipusPress.com

For the Ramparts.

"It wasn't an ischemic attack. It wasn't a seizure. You saw the x-rays . . . There was clearly something anterior to the larynx that looked like a laryngal sack. That's strictly simian. I obviously regressed! To some quasi-simian creature."

—Dr. Edward Jessup, *Altered States*

1

They revoke my Ph.D.

I had been practicing a questionable mode of pedagogy. I had been writing a toxic strain of theory.

Now I have to return the University so that I can get my degree back and salvage my identity.

Primordial.

2

Somebody attacks me at the front gate.

He reminds me of my dissertation advisor.

He is old and gray and sallow. And undeniably strong.

His bones converge into sharp angles and he looks more like an insect than an academic.

Upended on the grass, he hurls a large brick at my car and I swerve out of the way. He hurls another brick and I dodge it. He hurls one more brick and it lands on my windshield, splintering the glass like a broken equation.

I drive onto the grass and run over the old man.

3

I go to the Bursar's office to report the incident.

Nobody's in the office.

I leave a detailed note on the receptionist's desk and go to the Department.

Everything looks the same.

Somebody tells me what I have to do to reclaim my Ph.D. and they assign me a dormitory and a room and eighteen roommates.

I get my things from the car and move in.

Some of my roommates are academics, researchers and critics with revoked Ph.D.s. Others are regular college students. Primarily freshmen.

The freshmen are afraid of their peers. They aren't afraid of the former Ph.D.s and attempt to bully us. For the most part they succeed.

The freshmen think they can drink. The ex-Ph.D.s think they can drink.

They can't drink like me.

Drunk, I slam a bottle of Grey Goose into somebody's elapsed face.

It isn't an attempt to assert power. Somebody merely inflected their essence.

Nobody touches me after that. And when they speak to me, they never eyeball me. This may be a result of my artless aggression, social fallout from the extinction of culture, or a combination thereof. More and more, we lose the ability to interact with each other in person. Idle pleasantries become titanic hurdles.

It doesn't matter. I snap.

And I adapt.

From this point onwards, I incite fear and trembling in my roommates with the flair and enmity of a dystopian overlord.

There can be no other way.

As I often inform my students at the beginning of dense lectures: "The only things that move are the cold, wary eyes of the train."

5

The University's Continental Op pays us a visit. The geometry of his collar and lapel speaks to the algebra of his jaw.

He tells us that we have been put in the same room because the University is essentially bankrupt.

He tells us they can barely afford to squeeze eighteen of us in here even though we all have to pay for it.

Also, he notes, we are the lowest of the low: aborted Ph.D.s and inadequate standardized testers.

Finally he shouts, "Watch out!" Then he slams his fist into the wall. The blow leaves a mark.

When the Continental Op leaves, he closes the door gently, with a delicate click.

Nobody ever sees him again.

6

There are still two days before classes begin.

Bored and lonely, I go to a fraternity party.

They're shooting a pornographic film in the cafeteria.

They have sophisticated camera equipment. Flashbulbs pop like pillow-soft gunfire.

I was a member of this fraternity and I ate in this cafeteria and it has the same hybrid scent of stale beer and body odor and fried chicken.

I don't understand the porno.

"What is this?" I exclaim. "When I belonged to this fraternity we just got drunk, pulled down our pants and spanked each other with wooden paddles until our bottoms turned purple. For the love of God, I can see inside that young lady's pudendum. This is so . . . adult."

Everybody glares at me.

And I am reassured that the Universe does not want us to know what lurks beneath its skirt.

7

The Student Union is full of writers.

They all graduated from the University with B.A.s in creative writing, and M.A.s in creative writing, and M.F.A.s in creative writing, and some of them procured Ph.D.s in creative writing, despite the fact that an M.F.A. in creative writing is a terminal degree.

The writers come in all shapes and sizes and types. They are old and young. They are wise and naïve. They are grizzled and smooth. They are expectant and skeptical. They are rotund and withered. They possess countless varieties of crooked, yellow teeth.

Nobody will hire them. Nobody will represent them. Nobody will publish or buy their books.

Security tries to relegate them to the basement and the old wing. Technically they aren't allowed inside the Union. But they get inside no matter what anybody does.

One of the writers brushes up against me as I collect my mail.

Usually I don't care if people touch me. Students always liked to touch me, as if, somehow, it gave them access to my traumatic kernels.

In this instance, I get mad.

The writer senses it. He tries to run away.

I grab him by the neck with my strong hand.

I take a deep breath.

Pounding his face into the aluminum grid of mailboxes, I say, "Don't fucking touch me! Don't fucking touch me! Don't fucking touch me! Don't fucking touch me! Don't fucking touch me! Don't fucking touch me! Don't fucking touch me! Don't fucking touch me! Don't fucking touch me! Don't fucking touch me! Do not fucking touch me! Don't fucking touch me!"

The writer squirms and thrashes and blubbers and cries out for an administrator.

Nobody comes to his aid.

When I can't hear the writer anymore, and when he stops moving and wilts like an exorcised flower, I let him go.

8

It's the day before classes.

I've been sleeping well. My roommates are terrified of me and I insist on absolute silence when I'm in the room, day or night.

The storm sirens go off.

There's no storm. The President is about to give his welcome speech.

All of the students flow out of the dorms into the grassy hollow that the dorms and the halls and the observatories and the theaters and the athletic and teaching facilities surround like the stalagmites of a medieval crown.

They've set up a stage near the chapel. Slowly we congregate around it.

Onstage the Provost and the President of the University wait patiently for everybody to settle down. They're making smalltalk and then the President says, "God I love coitus. I just love it."

He doesn't know the microphone is on.

The Provost informs him about the microphone.

Immediately the President retracts the statement, but casually, as if he still doesn't know the microphone is on, ensuring everybody that, no matter what, he aspires to be the sort of patriarch and authority figure who lives and dies by the goodness of his Word. To the Provost he adds, "Who doesn't love coitus?"

Only the merit scholars hear him.

A lot of the students have dropped acid or eaten psychedelic mushrooms and are either petrified with fear or gibbering like chimps.

I'm somewhere between sobriety and drunkenness and I'm listening to a Walkman. Already I have reverted to my natural primitive state.

One of my roommates makes a commotion in the middle of the night and disturbs my sleep.

He misses his parents.

I had been dreaming about Hawaii. I vacationed on Maui and Oahu and the Big Island as a child, but I haven't gone back in years, confined to the liminal dustbowl of the Amerikan Midwest.

The older you get, the more tropics matter.

I turn on the lights and wake everybody up and sort of guarantee my roommates that I will kill them if I hear one more peep and so forth. I direct most of my aggression towards the homesick freshman, whose name is the same as mine, I discover. Then I turn off the lights and go back to sleep.

10

Instead of a dream, I experience a memory.

My only memory. The sole backstory of my character and identity. Everything else may or may not be a fiction.

The memory doesn't have anything to do with me. And yet everything hinges on it.

It goes like this:

A velour curtain of night slams into the grass.

My stepfather ambles onto the patio and stares into the middle distance. The weight of his jaw seems to tug on the bags of his eyes, drawing them into a grotesque pretense of mourning and absolution.

The stars come out. The sky is a scintillating dome.

There's a party inside the house. A family gathering. Maybe something else. Maybe nothing at all.

Somebody joins my stepfather on the patio. A young man with long teeth.

Smiling a tall smile, he glances back and forth between the middle distance and the sky and the aged man's face. My stepfather might know him.

"Beautiful night out," says the young man.

My stepfather grumbles something.

The young man looks at him hard and squints at the horizon. "What's out there?"

My stepfather grumbles something.

The tall smile wavers at the edges. The young man says, "Is something out there? Are we going to be ok? Why are you looking out there?"

There was a silence.

Then my stepfather says, "Because I fuckin' wanna look out there! Fuckhead!"

They continue to stare into the middle distance.

Soon my stepfather is alone again.

He stays that way until sunlight robs the distance of its precious interior.

11

I arrive at my first class fifteen minutes late.

Things happen fast.

The professor tries to cane me and I punch him and snatch his bamboo stick and beat him like a jungle monkey I'm trying to domesticate and all of the students whoop and cheer and they really love it.

After awhile I get kind of embarrassed for the professor and give him back the stick. I apologize for being tardy. "I was never tardy to classes I taught," I assure him, uncertain if this is true. "Well. Better to be absent than tardy, I always say. Nobody likes disruptions."

I sit next to an attractive young lady. She gives me a look and I give her a look and my endorphins retreat backstage and there is a hollow, abstemious sensation.

The ceiling panels fizz with electricity.

The professor gets up and tries to dust off his clothes and arrange himself into some semblance of presentablility.

He's a mess.

His shirt is untucked and his spectacles are flattened and broken and his belt isn't working and his hair and beard have converged into a feral, rumpled mass.

Clutching his waistband so his pants don't fall down, the professor gets in front of the class. He tries to introduce himself, then breaks down and cries.

He gives up. "It doesn't matter who I am or what I've done," he admits.

He hands out the syllabus.

As he reads through it, he breaks down and cries again. And again.

And again and again. Nine times, by my count. I ask the young lady next to me if this is accurate and she says she counted eight breakdowns.

The ceiling panels sound like they might explode.

I smile with one half of my face, invoking the attractive dimple. "What class is this?"

But somebody has told her about the other dimple, which is more like a scar than an insignia of promise and futurity. Otherwise she would have fallen under my power.

It is likely that everybody at the University knows about the other dimple now. I resolve never to smile again.

At some point the professor tells us we can go.

We go.

Nothing happens to the ceiling panels.

12

On the way to my next class, I stop by the library to see if, per my request, they have stocked copies of my latest book, a work of cultural theory.

The librarian says they ordered copies.

I don't believe her.

I look up the number and go to the stacks.

It's a big library and it takes me awhile to find the right aisle, but I can't get to where the book is supposed to be because somebody's shooting a porno.

I don't know if they're students, staff or faculty. They're young but they look old, or vice versa. Lots of body hair and imperfections of the skin. Decent muscle tone.

The film crew uses archaic camera equipment, clunky and heavy and loud, with massive flashbulbs that erupt like solar flares.

I wait for the scene to end. The protagonist has trouble with his extremity. The director keeps cutting to provide him with words of encouragement and dirty pictures to arouse him.

Resolute, I squeeze my way down the aisle to get to where my book should be.

The further I go, the more bodies press against me.

It's difficult to breathe.

I don't like this smell.

There is it. The book.

It's on the shelf behind the protagonist. If I'm careful I should be able to reach up and remove it without detection.

I reach for the book.

The protagonist makes a sound.

I reach for the book.

The protagonist makes another sound.

There's a commotion and everybody gets into position.

"Stop," I say, reaching for the book.

Nobody stops.

The protagonist makes another sound, seconds from accomplishing the proverbial College Try.

I can't reach the book.

Unwilling to play the rabble-rouser, I escape the pornographers and flee the library so that I can get to class on time. I don't want to make a habit out of turning my professors into spectacles of pathos.

13

Redundancy is the only viable reality. Sometimes we may substitute "redundancy" with "recurrence."

I go to the rest of my classes and the day threads into weeks and the weeks thread into months.

14

The semester (un)folds like an origami in flames.

15

After I finish my last exam, I remember that I have a family. A wife and kids. I blame the epistemological slippage on memory and especially history. As I articulate in my first book, a manifesto intended to both counter and facilitate a certain Icelandic philosopher's "aesthetic of impertinence," "History is that which hides in the deepest graves of our brainyards and dies for good the moment we try to exhume it."

I call my wife.

"Wrong number."

I try another number.

"Wrong number."

I try another one.

It's ringing.

It's ringing.

It's ringing.

It's still ringing.

"Hello?"

"Wife?"

"Who's this?"

"It's me."

"Oh."

We have a conversation.

"But your temper," she concludes.

"Temper. Right."

"Also, you don't understand me. You don't even know what I want. You haven't asked. I'm not going to ask you for something you can't give."

"Give. Want. Understand. Yes."

My youngest daughter gets on phone. She sounds happy.

"Daddy! Daddy! Last night I had a nightmare about the shadow of the moon! I miss you." She begins to cry. I tell her it'll be ok—there are no such things as shadows of the moon.

I decide to spend the holidays on campus, in my dorm room, alone, smoking clove cigarettes, drinking green tea and red wine, and doing push-ups, sit-ups, and chin-ups. I quit smoking years ago but cloves aren't like real cigarettes and I only inhale them during moments of extreme anxiety.

16

Before the holiday break, I am required to visit with an academic advisor to discuss my progress.

He's about twenty years younger than me.

He's overweight. He's unattractive. He's going bald on top.

"All bald spots are guilty-looking," I note.

"Pardon me?"

I don't think he maintains a healthy diet. I ask him if he works out and he says no.

"So how have things been going?" says the academic advisor, studying my papers.

"All right."

"I see that you got an A in astronomy. That's good."

"Thank you. I like stars and nebulas and so forth."

"You also got an A in business mathematics. Well done."

"Thank you. I like percentages and amortization schedules and all that."

"Well it looks like you got As in all of your classes. That's a 4.0 grade point average."

"I'm not altogether sure I needed to take most of those classes. Any of them, in fact. My Ph.D. is in a very particular field, although I am not particular myself."

"Don't worry about that. Everybody has to take electives and core courses. Or retake them, as it were. You'll be fine. Just keep doing what you're doing."

I nod.

"Well everything looks good. Good grades are a good sign. Any questions or concerns? How has college life been treating you?"

"Very well," I confess. "I must say that I don't like my roommates or my professors or the hall monitors and janitors or anybody really. But I have become an expert in the pornographic industry. Everywhere I go there's something new to learn. I had forgotten how much college students enjoy fornication. Give young people a taste of modern technology and there's no stopping them. I've seen more copulation in real life at the University than any magazine could ever hope to show me. There are so many kinds I don't even know where to start. Transsexual porn is just the beginning of Vanilla Death. There's Darjeeling porn. Buckwheat porn. Refrigerator porn. Entropy porn. Diglossia porn. Black supremacy porn. Arch-donkey porn. Evil genie porn. Apornal porn. No-bones-or-joints-in-corpses porn. Synchronic analytical dithyrambic bad motherfucker porn. So forth. You know. There's, like, everything. The list is truly endless. There are formal, scientific names for all of these subgenres. But who cares about names? The sky's the limit. In addition, I have begun a new research project based on my rereading of a so-called 'forgotten' Greek mathematician whose algorithms and *modes de vie* have presented themselves to me in a new light. I can barely sleep I'm so excited about it; the moment unconsciousness threatens to extinguish me, I stumble upon another idea and have to turn on the light and write it down. My brain is an electromagnetic earthfucker. Furthermore, my bench press has exceeded 300 pounds. That's a lot of weight for an ectomorph, not to mention an academic."

I remember that I'm no longer an academic. It hurts me.

"Let's see what else. I haven't made many friends, but I don't want any friends, and I don't like people because people just get in the way with their bodies and their words and so forth. I just want to do my work. I'm a bit of a stereotype that way. I was a stereotype, I mean. But I'm adjusting to the reality of my situation."

"It sounds like you're adjusting," says the academic advisor, putting my papers aside. "I'm glad."

"I'm glad you're glad."

We wait for something to happen.

I say, "Is there anything else?"

"I guess not."

I think he's going to say something. He doesn't.

He's scared of me, I think.

I have large biceps with big veins, but I try not to hold my arms at ninety-degree angles so as to diminish the swell of my vascularity. I have a tendency to overtrain.

17

Despite myself, I miss my roommates over the break.

I go to the Union to get a coffee and a bagel and contemplate the fate of the noösphere.

A writer stops me in the entranceway and asks if I will look at his manuscript. "It took me, like, five years to write this book," he assures me. "I think you'll really like it. Enjoy!"

I grab him by the neck and slam his head into the wall. "Fuck your book! Fuck your book! Fuck your book! Fuck your book! Fuck your book! Fuck your book! Fuck your book! Fuck your book! Fuck your book! Fuck your book! Fuck your fucking book! Fuck your book!"

During my diatribe the writer tries to bite me. I keep a firm grip and I keep yelling and slamming his head into the wall until he loses consciousness and flops over.

In the Union café, I decide to order a turkey wrap instead of a bagel. Less carbs, more protein, although processed meats are high in sodium, which retains water in the body and is bad for the heart.

18

Two years pass like refried dreams.

A lot happens.

For instance:

I develop a meaningful relationship with the R.A. in my dorm. It collapses.

I develop a meaningful relationship with my psych professor. It collapses.

I develop a meaningful relationship with the President of the University. It collapses.

I develop a meaningful relationship with at least six of my roommates. They all collapse before they ever happen.

I develop a meaningful relationship with several members of the opposite sex. They never happen.

I realize that relationships are doomed to entropy and failure. I don't talk to anybody for months unless a professor calls on me in class or I get drunk and call my wife and kids or a writer gets too close to me.

More happens.

And more. Two years is a long time no matter how you quantify and experience it.

For instance:

I get a part-time job at the library to supplement my income from book sales and help pay for my (re)new(ed) Ph.D. The job involves data entry and various organizational skills and techniques. Payment is a partial tuition waiver and a modest stipend.

On my first day I walk into the head librarian's office. Nobody's there.

Somebody left a note on the desk.

"The laminator in the learning center is broke," reads the note.

I go to the learning center to see what's happening with the laminator.

There are several ex-Ph.D.s I recognize from one of my classes trying to figure out how to use "the Internet." They're huddled around an old computer, one of those dirty, ochre-colored Apples with the green numerals and the cubed miniscreen that sits atop a hard drive the size of an anvil.

"What's the problem with the laminator?" I ask.

They don't know.

"Well it's broke. Broken. It's not working."

They don't know what a laminator is.

I'm not sure I do either.

"Well where is it then? I'll give it a shot."

The ex-Ph.D.s shrug. They've forgotten what I'm talking about and they want to know what I'm talking about.

I find what I think might be the laminator and take it apart. There are how-to-dismantle directions taped to the door of the cabinet beneath it, but I don't care for the tedium of reading through directions, and I always try to do things myself first, even if it means botching the job beyond repair.

This apparatus appears to be a heated roll laminator with all of the trimmings and fixings. I understand how it works immediately, instinctively. Heat rollers melt glue onto a lamination film that is subsequently applied to a paper-based substrate by pressure rollers. I don't understand the purpose of the machine. I calculate that it has something to do with the unbridled embellishment or protection of printed documents.

I see the problem.

I tell the ex-Ph.D.s to hand me a Phillips screwdriver.

They observe me.

I get a Phillips screwdriver and remove what I believe to be a rogue screw.

No. It's not a rogue screw. It belongs where it is.

I screw the screw back in and toss the screwdriver aside. Then I remove the micro-adjustable slitter assembly unit, which looks suspicious.

There is a thermal response.

I remove a few casters and place them on a table. I remove a few mandrels and drop them on the floor. I gut the entire laminator and throw the viscera in the garbage.

"I don't know what's wrong with this shit-wheeling contraption!" I divulge, kicking over the laminator.

Curiously, the ex-Ph.D.s have managed to access the Internet on the old Apple. The porn is green and it's in 8-bit. It takes awhile to load, but it still looks pretty good.

19

The University is embossed in trees. The Office of the Provost is in the nicest building on campus. All of the administration buildings exhibit a gothic beauty that flirts with the Kantian sublime, unlike the instructional buildings, which are essentially tenements, lanky and oxidized and in some cases rubbled. Because of low wages, most faculty can't afford rent and must live in their offices, often with their families; laundry streams out of the windows on frayed lengths of twine. Administrators, on the other hand, enjoy unlimited creature comforts, ranging from high ceilings and Scandinavian furniture to walk-in humidors and spitshined bidets in every bathroom.

I need to talk to the Provost to find out how long it's going to take to get my Ph.D. back. Nobody told me. I assume a certain span of time will have to elapse.

I don't know what the Provost's job entails.

At the institution that retrograded me, the Provost's job entailed lumbering around the cafeteria and commenting on people's food. He did this all day, every day.

His motives remain uncertain. All I can be sure of is that he enjoyed the poststructuralization of food.

If the Provost eyeballed a meal that intrigued him, he proceeded to deconstruct it with Derridean rigor, and he even employed Derridean rhetoric during moments of special excitement or angst, reducing the food to a mere figment, an effigy of its former self. By the time he had finished, you couldn't help feeling badly for the food, as if it were a living, sentient organism, wrongfully punished, robbed of its precious ignorance, aware for the first time in its life that it was a voided, vacuous superzero.

While my experience with Provosts is limited, I assume that most Provosts have duties beyond the scope of antagonizing food and, by extension, the people who eat it.

One of my elderly roommates had told me that the Provost at the University would be able to apprise me of my standing and future as a student. The roommate is an ex-Ph.D. too. I didn't take his advice seriously. If I didn't know anything about Provosts, how would he know anything about Provosts? My underclass roommates didn't even know what a Provost was. They accused me of making the word up. As I beat them, I realized "Provost" was indeed a strange word. I looked it up in the OED.

Etymology: Originally post-classical Latin *propositus*; subsequently reinforced by the Anglo-Norman *provolt*, *provot*, *provout*, Anglo-Norman and Old French *provost* chief magistrate in an area (c. 1090 in Old French), chief dignitary of a collegiate church (c. 1174), the archangel Michael as leader of the heavenly host (c. 1174), the commander of a legion (1272 or earlier in Anglo-Norman), reeve, steward (a. 1377 or earlier), overseer (14th cent. or earlier). Post-classical Latin *propositus* prior or abbot (6th cent.; from 8th cent. in British sources), reeve of a manor (from 9th cent. in British sources), reeve of a borough (c. 1280 in a British source), head of a college or university (1457 in a British source in *propositus collegii*), alteration of classical Latin *praepositus* PREPOSITUS *n.* Old English had also *prafost* (directly classical Latin *praepositus* PREPOSITUS *n.*), used interchangeably with *profost* (it is probably only accidental that the former is attested, but the latter is not, in sense 4a).

I decide it won't hurt to at least visit the Provost, if only to discover what tasks he performs on a daily basis.

The only person I encounter as I enter Recitation Hall and walk up two hundred marble stairs to the Provost's office is a student who has gotten tired climbing the stairway and sat down to rest and have lunch. I stop and talk to her for awhile and pour us two small glasses of Malbec from the wine tote I carry around. I teach her about the assorted flavors in the wine and how to detect them with different parts of your mouth. We have another few glasses. I run out of wine and she asks me if I want to go play Frisbee golf. I tell her that would be nice but I have to go talk to the Provost first about something.

"Wait here."

Upstairs I have a similar interaction with the Provost's secretary, who is drinking a glass of wine at her desk. I introduce myself as the Dean of the College of Something-or-Other and I inform her regretfully about my lack of wine. She gets another glass out of the drawer and gives me a liberal pour. We discuss what she likes best about the accoutrements in the ladies room and about how students are irrevocable nuisances and we keep drinking and drinking and exchanging pleasantries until her wine is gone.

"Excuse me."

As she stands I kind of take her in my arms and play with her ears, but she pushes herself away and with a coy giggle runs down the hallway to the ladies room, heels clacking against the crystal floor.

I enter the Provost's office.

He's sitting behind a stately, elevated, custom-made desk playing a long Pan pipe.

He stops playing it. "Yes?" He glances at me, at his lap, behind himself, then back at me. "Yes?" he reiterates.

On the desktop is a medieval goblet.

"What are you drinking?" I inquire.

He frowns. "Wine. Chardonnay."

I wince.

He lifts the goblet with two hands and takes a dirty sip. "Who the hell are you?"

I tell him who I am. The Provost shakes his head.

I walk across the office and sit in a chair on the other side of the desk. It takes me about 15 seconds to get there. I can't see him because his desk is too tall and the chair is normal-sized and hence too short.

I get up and stand on the chair. Now I can see him.

"Are you standing on the chair? Please don't stand on the chair."

I step off the chair. I don't sit down.

I can see him.

"Who are you, sir?"

I remind him.

"What can I do for you?"

It takes me about an hour to explain my situation. It shouldn't take this long. My situation is cut and dry: I was In, then I was Out, and now I need to know how long it will take me to get back In. But when I talk at length to administrators I deploy a lot of techno-jargon and magniloquence.

The Provost goes through nearly two bottles of Chardonnay during my monologue. He offers me a glass on at least six occasions. I don't drink white wine and politely decline the offer every time, with the same response, and the same expression, in the same tone: "No thank you. I don't care for white wine."

At last I say, "How long will it take?"

The Provost doesn't know. He doesn't think anybody will know. He thinks it's rather strange that I had my Ph.D. taken away in the first place. He's never heard of such a thing. Even stranger, he thinks, is that I returned to college to get the Ph.D. back. "Is this common praxis in the industry?"

I scrutinize his obtuse eyes. They're not bloodshot, but something's wrong with them. "You never leave your office, do you."

He peers around the office.

I leave the office.

The girl on the stairs is still there. She passed out.

I sit down next to her and watch her sleep for awhile, admiring the tilt of her eyebrows. Then I wake her up and we go play Frisbee golf. It's fun. I win.

20

When somebody cuts me, I bleed syntax.

I might say this aloud: "Why is every young lady who attends or works at the University named Shorty? Even the tall ones."

"Shawty," somebody replies.

"What?"

"Shawty. S. H. A. W. T. Y."

I turn up the volume on my Walkman.

Metaphysics.

Translation: science that is aware of itself as such.

This certificate of existence hemorrhages like a stuck thunderpig. It loses momentum the moment it begins to pick up speed. Reality is only real by way of the art of misperception and disavowal. I will be the first human being to live forever. All of the (Big) Others will do likewise. Muscle memory is an illusion as memory in general, corporeal or cognitive, is deceitful, if not treacherous; ultimately that flexed bicep has nothing to compare itself to, no prototype, no former, weaker, less vascular embodiment to scrutinize in the mirror. All old, expensive colleges do the same thing: the sharp tips of their administration buildings and church spires tear holes in the sky that relinquish the goat's milk of Paradise. These observations transcend mere exuberance. As a child I enjoyed moments of isolation and lackluster cant. Tabula rasa. I own eight Bunsen burners, twenty-six abacuses, forty-one protractors, and a deranged Grizzly bear. Tabula rasa. I avoid anaphora and aporia like the plague. And yet they plague me. In mind. On paper.

I have prelapsarian tendencies.

Viz., I am a firm and sagacious believer in the narrative of failure.

Narrative as thoroughbred fiction. Narrative as lived experience. Narrative as desire and production and the death of meaning.

I have been told that my rictus grin reminisces a scar. This scar is essentially a toolkit for existence.

It takes a long time to figure out how machinery works, but once you accomplish a rudimentary understanding of the machinery, you are in a good position to break that machinery. It doesn't matter if you put it back together. The option for destruction lingers like a forsaken ovule.

As the reviews editor for a prominent academic journal, I receive many queries.

As a human being, I receive many queries.

Even when I retreat to liminal, would-be secure interstices, the queries continue to roll in.

It is my privilege and my duty not to answer anybody.

Unlike rhetorical devices, answers are overrated.

Answer a question and sooner or later another question will air its dirty laundry.

22

I am in class now.

Intro to Film Studies, I think.

Nobody's listening to the professor. The content of his lecture is too hard, or too boring, or too Old Hat, or too irrelevant, or too verbatim from the textbook.

As always, I am sitting in the back, in the corner, by the window, staring into Oblivion.

A man turns to me and introduces himself as Bill.

Bill isn't sitting in a seat.

He's standing near the window, as if banished there.

Has he been standing there the whole time? Or did he get out of his seat during the lecture and sneak beside me?

He's undernourished.

He's middle-aged.

He's wearing a tweed coppola.

He reminds me of Andy Capp. My grandfather used to love that comic strip.

I inform Bill about my grandfather's deep and reverent penchant for Andy Capp.

Bill is polite enough. I stand up and we shake hands and talk about the weather.

The professor gives us the evil eye.

I return the act of aggression with a look that says GO FUCK YOURSELF OR I'll KILL YOU!!!

The professor understands. His book on astro-pragmatics was ridiculous. I wrote a scathing article in protest and critique of it just three years ago. The article met with terrific acclaim and more or less tanked his career.

The evil-eye melts into his skull.

Bill and I converse in very confident yet very reserved tones. I learn that he spent some time in Hawaii.

"I've spent time there too. Do you like poi?"

He tells me he's Hawaiian.

"Oh. Do you like the Brothers Cazimero?"

He reminds me that he's Hawaiian.

"Oh. Have you stayed at the Royal Hawaiian? The pink palace on Waikiki Beach. It's the oldest hotel on Oahu, right? I used to stop there every year on my way to Kyoto. My kids came along sometimes. They loved it. I can't remember if my wife accompanied us. You can't believe the breakfasts they served at the Royal Hawaiian. All fresh fruit. Then, after breakfast, me and the girls would go surfing. There's a coral reef in the bay, though, like a rhizome of knives, and we couldn't wipe out; if we wiped out and fell in the water, the reef would tear us to pieces. So nobody wiped out. We became expert surfers instantly. Had the reef not been there, had it been safe to surf, and if falling off of the board would not have entailed certain death, it probably would have taken us weeks, perhaps months to learn how. I may have never learned. There's something to be said for epistemo-logical prudence."

Bill says, "I'm not sure if prudence is the right word."

I say, "No? Well something like that. Anyway you should check out the Royal Hawaiian. I'd live there if I could. I—"

"Do you like pornographic films?" interrupts Bill.

I cock my head. "Do I like what?"

"Pornos. You know." Bill makes a gesture that, I gauge, represents what a pornographic film involves.

"Do I like pornos?"

Bill narrows his eyes.

"It doesn't matter if I like them or not. I watch them, if that's what you mean. I'm alive, aren't I?"

Bill tells me he's an independent filmmaker in addition to a student. He tells me he sees something in me, some kind of charisma or energy.

I inform him that I'm perfectly aware of my raw Benjaminian aura.

Bill wonders if I'd like to star in this docu-porno he wants to make about contemporary college life.

I explain that I really only enjoy pornography in private life, whether I'm involved in it or merely standing on the sidelines. Also, his idea isn't terribly unique.

Ignoring the latter assertion, Bill tries to convince me that public sex, and the dissemination of public sex, is a good thing.

Uninterested in "good things," I cut him off and underscore how I'm not passing judgment on pornography and have no moral objection to it. "My concerns are purely subjective. They belong to me alone."

We discuss what specifically constitutes pornography and the dynamics thereof.

"Surely just having sex in public isn't pornographic," Bill remarks. "And yet if other people can see what's going on, then it becomes pornographic, doesn't it. Pornography is pornography because of the gaze of the other, isn't it."

I want to go back to talking about Hawaii and the Brothers Cazimero. Their song "The Pueo, Tara & Me," about an owl, really stuck with me. Sometimes it makes me cry if I think about it too much. If I listen to it, I'll definitely cry. But I don't want to make a stink about our discussion of pornography. Bill clearly wants to talk about it. As is often the case with people I am not inclined to beat, I allow him to take the discursive reigns and acclimatize to the direction, the speed, the tonality of his interlocution, chiming in at key moments with sighs of affirmation, with engaged modulations, and sometimes I respond outright, but no more than a sentence or two at a time, and after awhile I can tell that Bill is really enjoying himself.

At some point, the professor stops lecturing and just stares blankly at us. So do all of the other students.

I turn to the professor. "Do you harbor fantasies of dismemberment? Do any of you?" I look around the room. Most of the other students look away. The students that don't—I keep my eyes on them, one at a time, until they look away too.

When I turn back to Bill, he's gone. I never see him again.

23

Apropos dismemberment . . .

My field of interest—although not my field of specialty—is the grotesque. Who isn't interested in the grotesque? Either it repels you or it attracts you. Either way it interests you.

Thus everybody's field of interest is the grotesque.

Here are some terms we might associate with it:

Lowly.

Earthly.

Uncanny.

Male bodily fluids.

Zoomorphology.

Kristeva: Abjection. That which is cast off. That which wallows in the dirt like the memory of a dead soul.

Lacan: *Crasse!*

OED: "Picturesquely irregular. Fantastically absurd."

Dryden: "An hideous Figure of their Foes they drew, Nor Lines, nor Looks, nor Shades, nor Colours true; And this Grotesque design, expos'd to Publick view."

Finally, Bakhtin [to a lover]: "I don't like your mouth. That gaping aperture unnerves me. That wide-open bodily abyss reminds me of your anus. And I prefer your anus.

Copulation, defecation, mastication—these perfectly terrific and disgusting enactments constitute the same prenumbra. All of them grope the sordid privates of the beginning and the end of life simultaneously."

My parents come to see me. They supported me during my first *voyage dans la lune* in graduate school. Naturally they want to see how I'm holding up the second time around.

The first thing they do when they come into my dorm room is turn on all the lights and open all the window curtains. "You need light, son," my father explains. "We come from light, you know."

"We come from wombs. *Uteri*. Uteri are dark. Coffins of flesh and tubes and moisture."

It's early. Even the ex-Ph.D.s are asleep. Some of them are in their early 60s. Everybody sort of groans and I snap at them to keep quiet and pull the covers over their heads and lay still. My parents are elderly. This instance of bawdy aggression makes my parents nervous and fitful. I assure them that everything is ok, that my roommates and I have a special relationship.

"For instance," I explain, "last week I decreed that they couldn't look me directly in the eyes. If they do, I beat them real good. Sometimes I just put them in the closet for a few hours." I point at the closet and snap my fingers. The door opens and a head pokes out. I snap my fingers again and the head disappears, the door closes. "In theory I don't have a problem with my roommates looking at me. It's the principle of it. Hence our special relationship."

"I understand," says Dad.

Mom starts cleaning things up. I order her to stop. "The more you try to dispose of trash in a dorm room, the faster it accumulates."

"He's right," says Dad.

I put on a tie and we go out to eat.

The restaurant is crowded and there's an agglomeration of townies in the lobby. They just got out of church. Or they're on their way. The men wear lint-ridden sweater vests that leak crinkled shirttails. The women wear funny hats and cheap mother-of-the-bride uniforms that accentuate the worst parts of their physiques.

I push through the throng, dragging my parents behind me, and confront the hostess. She stands behind a podium like a doe that's about to be slaughtered. She's holding a bunch of menus and she doesn't seem to know what to do with them. I think she's in my econometrics class. I ask her what the fuck's going on with all of the people and so forth. She says she doesn't know and I say, "What the fuck is happening! How much fucking longer do we have to fucking wait! Give me the information! FUUUCK!!!"

"Son," says Dad, placing a hand on my shoulder.

I feel badly, but that doesn't change my attitude. Nor does it change this simple human fundament: parents incite adamant regression.

I berate the waitress for awhile. Then the manager or somebody managerial-looking comes out. He apologizes and seats us. On the way to the table, I assure my parents that you got to take the reigns before they're even tethered to the sleigh. It's the only way to ensure that things get done the way you want them done.

We sit in a booth. Me on one side, my parents on the other side.

Now the hard part.

Buffet or menu?

I don't remember what I decide on. Maybe the menu because I don't go up to the buffet and I end up getting a bunch of food.

During the meal I forget my parents are there.

The book I'm working on right now is harrowing me. It's all I can think about. I can't sleep. I can't study. The flows of my desire shoot in awkward directions.

My thesis is devolving like a Morlock. I don't know why.

I spread all of my notes across the table and try to figure out what's wrong as I drink my coffee and eat my poached eggs and my turkey sausage patties and my demitasse of mixed fruit.

"Son," says Dad.

I look across the table and remember that my parents came to visit. They're sitting there shoulder-to-shoulder like two wrinkled children who have been sent to the principal's office. "Oh. I'm sorry, parents. What was I thinking. Let me put this away."

It takes me about 10 minutes to get all of my papers and things back into my satchel—about half of the time, I gauge, it took me to get everything out. And I must have poured over my notes for a good 30 minutes. I wonder what my parents did while I was working. I lose track of time when I'm working. I don't think I heard their voices. I'm pretty sure they didn't have anything to eat. I would have noticed (i.e., remembered) if they slid in and out of the booth a few times to go to the buffet table. I want to ask them, but I'm admittedly embarrassed and I don't want to call attention to the fact that I forgot about them. As an only child, my cognizance and affections mean everything to my parents.

The mere suggestion that I "lost" them—even though they witnessed me "lose" them—would be a demoralizing blow, no matter how I structured my discourse.

When in doubt: deflect.

"I got an A in my Frisbee class last term," I brag. "It met five times a week at 8 a.m. and I showed up every day and I was never tardy. I can accomplish just about any Frisbee throw known to mankind. And I was voted MVP on my ultimate Frisbee team."

Mom reaches across the table and touches my arm. "Honey, are you all right?"

I look at her hand and think about the question. "Yeah. Yes. I'm ok." I reconsider the question. "I mean, I'm lonely, I guess. And I'm mad. Of course I'm mad. I was mad before they sent me back here. You know. Once you get to a certain point in your life, you can't retool the circuitry, right?" I clear my throat. "It's ok though. I'm ok. I mean, I'm sad, I'm dejected, I'm agitated, I'm rancorous, I'm resentful, I'm hateful, I'm unflappable, I'm hostile, I'm ridiculous, I'm blue, I'm pathological, I'm crepuscular, I'm tyrannical, I'm confused, I'm maleficent, I'm fanatical, I'm bushwhacked, I'm moravaginean, I'm *non est hic*, I'm . . . I was going to say uxorious, but I'm not that. The kids are all right, though, I think." I pause. Nod. "Everything's fine. I'm anti-oedipal and my muscles are very hard and big and vascular for a guy my age. That's all that matters."

My parents try to pay for the check. I say something like get the hell outta here and give the waitress my credit card. She takes the card and stares at the card and stares at me and stares at the card again and you just know she knows there's no money on it. Still, she goes through the motions. In a few minutes she returns to the table and gives me back my card and blinks at me expectantly.

"There's no money on it," I explain.

As always, Mom cries when we part ways and Dad gives me a stiff handshake. I return the handshake, then lean in and give him a hug. It surprises him. But after awhile he de-stiffens and eventually he drapes an arm over me and hugs me back.

25

I quit my job. I don't tell anybody. It's too much work anyway and I have other things to do.

For years, I continue to receive a stipend as well as a partial tuition waiver.

It's not enough.

I should have asked my parents for some money when they were here. Book sales are weak these days.

One of my publishers has stopped sending me royalties. I don't remember receiving any royalties from them in the first place. I check my records. The records say I never received one royalty check from them, although they did give me a sizable advance.

That was eight years ago.

Even after I bully and extort my roommates and some other people living in my dorm and a few other dorms and faculty residences, I don't have enough money.

Granted, money is relative. What seems like a little to me will doubtless be a lot to somebody else.

I have expensive tastes and was raised with bourgeois ethics notwithstanding my grasp of the concept of humility.

I call my wife.

I ask her to sell one of the kids and send me the cash.

She gets mad.

I tell her I'm just kidding. That's the truth. But I want to see how she'll react just the same.

She reacts.

I say, "I love you."

She says something back and then we hang up.

26

Somebody parks a Ford Excursion on the lawn in front of the Union. Several writers have gathered around it. They study and comment on it as if they've never seen a car before. I don't blame them. It's big.

Too big.

The writers see me coming and disperse like a pack of frightened rodents.

I press my nose against the driver's side window of the Ford Excursion and look inside.

It's dirty.

Empty soda cans. Cigarette butts and ash. Wrappers and old clothes and dirt and dust.

The driver's in the car. Observing me.

"Get this thing outta here you fuckin' dummy," I say.

He blinks at me.

He tells me to go to hell or something.

I go inside the Union and get all of the janitors.

I round them up like so much livestock.

They're reluctant to follow my lead but I promise them various IOUs and rewards and even raises that I of course lack the desire or the authority to deliver.

Standing on a table in the café, I give a kind of neomarxist motivational speech, gesticulating like Nietzsche after a bad meal. Then we go outside.

We lean against the Ford Excursion and start to push.

The driver goes crazy.

He yells and spits and swears and kicks and punches the window and the dash and the roof and the steering wheel as we push the Ford Excursion onto its flipside and then push it back onto its rightside.

We do it again.

Again.

Until the Ford Excursion idles in the street, upside-down, where it should be.

I say, "No parking on the lawn!"

The janitors clap. One of them cheers. The other janitors look at him as if he's done something wrong. He has, in a way. Nobody else cheered . . .

The janitor who cheered shoves his hands into his pockets and stares at his shoes. Like his sense of etiquette, they need polishing.

Christmas break!

I don't want to go home.

I stay at the University.

Somebody sends me a check. I look at the box. I don't look at the name or address of the sender.

I cash the check and get the money.

My clothes are getting old.

I go to the University bookstore to buy some shirts and pants and some textbooks for the upcoming semester.

All they sell are t-shirts and sweatshirts with the words HEY SHAWTY! on them.

The only pants available are sweatpants.

I buy a few pairs of sweatpants and some sequined HEY SHAWTY! t-shirts and sweatshirts.

I go back to my room.

I throw out my old clothes and put on the new ones.

Most of adult life is spent discovering the mystery of how very little you matter.

29

On the care of the body . . .

I don't like hair.

My hair.

The hair on my body.

I shed. Hence I shave.

From nose to toe.

I use grooming shears.

I don't shave down to the skin. I like to maintain a veneer of fuzz so that I don't resemble a shrew or an outpatient. This is important to me.

Many things are important to me.

My forearms are the hardest to trim because of the bones in my wrist and my elbow. I always make mistakes and cut the hair too close. If there are too many patches I shave my forearms to the skin with a straight razor.

Sometimes I throw out my grooming shears and get a new pair, thinking it'll be easier.

It's never easier.

Nothing's ever easier, it seems.

All grooming sheers present unique problems.

There's simply no good way to shave my forearms.

Thankfully I don't have any hair on my back except for a few nearly invisible strands on my lower, outer flanks that are easily plucked or shaved if I look over my shoulder in the mirror.

I can feel myself getting rounder.

31

And flatter.

Like a manhole.

33

Wedged into the asphalt. Sleeping and dreaming beneath the vermilion sky.

Abstraction.

35

The academic ideological apparatus interpellates all of us.

For academics and non-academics alike, there is no escaping the apparatus.

Hence I have conceived of a new book-length project in which I will explore the vicissitudes of the word "baby" in pop songs. Every singer pronounces the word in a distinctive, utterly singular way. They employ different inflections for divergent purposes and at times devious ends. It confounds me that a study of this nature has never been conducted before, if only by a linguist. But there's nothing out there.

Nothing.

36

Sometimes, when I am revising my manuscripts, I forget to breath. My roommates have to remind me. I don't like it. I don't like them to talk at all. But they see my face go red and then gray and finally purple and despite how much they hate me they can't shoulder the burden of my potential death. Stockholm Syndrome.

Some of them enjoy it when I flog them.

One of them asks for it.

I don't enjoy flogging people. Not for any reason. But the Law is the Law and somebody must uphold it.

I use a cat o' nine tails that I purchased as a Boy Scout. I can't remember where I purchased it. But I had my uniform on when I gave the cashier my bills and coins.

I never stop flogging my roommates until I draw blood and they are sufficiently terrorized, i.e., happy.

37

I got to go to the bank.

I got to get some money from the money machine.

I put in my card and press the buttons and wait and press the buttons and wait and wait and wait and my money comes out of the slit.

I take it, count it.

The money blows away. It's windy.

I go inside the bank to get reimbursed. The teller gives me a hard time. She has to talk to her supervisor. They go back and forth and the supervisor makes a phone call. They look at each other. They look at me.

They decide to reimburse me.

I count my money as I exit the bank.

When I step outside, the money blows out of my hands. The wind has picked up.

I go back inside the bank to get reimbursed and the teller sort of laughs at me and her supervisor comes out and laughs at me and they call somebody on the phone and I can hear them laughing really loud on the other end of the line.

I'm persistent.

My persistence wears everybody out. They reimburse me just to get rid of me, although I'm careful to explain that I'm not breaking the law, that I didn't do anything wrong, that I can't help it if the forces of nature are against me, against all of us, and finally that I resent the allegation, veiled or otherwise, that I'm trying to take advantage of the bank and get away with something. Apologizing like henpecked spouses, the bank staff nod perfunctorily and they dole out idle reassurances and they call me sir and so forth and I back out of the bank staring at everybody with my jaw flexed and my eyes round and wet and insane.

This time I'm careful to hold on tightly to my money in two fists.

I'm angry now.

I don't like those people in the bank.

I might have had too much to drink earlier.

I can't hold my liquor anymore.

I may just relax the muscles in my fingers.

I may just loosen my fists a hair so that the wind can rob me a third time.

Nothing happens. The wind has died a quiet death.

I open my hands and the money falls onto the sidewalk between my feet.

I stand there for awhile, like a soldier at ease, observing the crisp bills and wondering if the wind will rise from the grave and do something.

Nothing happens.

Somebody comes up to me.

They see me looking down at the money.

They look back and forth between my face and the money and my face and the money.

They bend over.

They take the money.

They run away.

I run into the bank. "Did you see that!"

Nobody saw anything.

Getting reimbursed a third time is difficult but not impossible. It never is. Given enough time, the patience, temperament, and psychological endurance of the human condition will always run its course.

"At any rate," I explain to the teller, singling her out, "why would I lie?"

38

"I want to declare my intent to go up for tenure," I say. "Do I have to put it in writing or is my word good enough?"

"You are a student, if I'm not mistaken," responds the chairperson of the Promotion and Tenure committee, a lumbering man with off-kilter shoulders and a beard he keeps to conceal a deep cleft palate.

"Yes. I suppose."

"Students can't go up for tenure. They aren't eligible." He touches his overlip.

"I received tenure before, though. And I have all of the requisite publications." I hand him my curriculum vita and a copy of my latest book. "Generally my work has been positively reviewed in all of the major journals in my field of study. There have been a few bad reviews, but they were written exclusively by scholars whose ideas I turned inside-out, exposing their idiot cores."

The chairperson makes bird noises as he peruses my c.v. and skims through my book. "Impressive," he concludes, touching his overlip again. I'm beginning to think that it's a nervous tic. "But as I said, students can't go up for tenure. You are a student."

I flex my jaw. "I can see your deformity." I point at his face. "Your cleft palate. There. I can see it. That beard isn't hiding anything."

Sighing, the chairperson smiles a crooked smile. "What a relief. I was trying to get you to notice it." Once again he touches his overlip. "Sometimes people forget to say anything. I keep meaning to shave but I never get around to it."

We shake hands before I leave.

39

I wander around for awhile. I don't think I talk to anybody and I may or may not go to class. The moon flitters on and off like an ailing lamp. I use toilets frequently, even when I don't have to go. I don't stop wandering until I have used every toilet in every public building at the University.

40

After all these years it occurs to me that I have retaken all of my undergraduate classes. I didn't need to do that. Did I?

I go to talk to a student advisor.

She's a woman. She's attractive. She's younger than me.

"How old are you?" I ask.

"At least fifteen years younger than you," she retorts. "Maybe more."

I nod. My underlip tries to outmaneuver my overlip.

Balking, I say, "Do you like my shirt?" I push out my chest and admire the logo. "Technically I may call you shawty, correct? Or is there an age limit? How old does a woman have to be before a man is no longer allowed to call her shawty? Can somebody's grandmother be called shawty without it sounding acerbic, juvenile, or downright pejorative? Can I call a skeleton shawty as long as it possessed female genitals when it was encrusted in flesh? How does it work? What has happened to the sphere of culture and oblivion that interpellates us? Why is there no linguistic counterpart for shawty in the male register? I assume it has to do with patriarchy and the nature of power relations, but it's dangerous to assume anything. Perhaps shawty is not gendered at all. I have never heard a woman call a man shawty. I have never heard a woman call a woman shawty. I have never heard a man call a man shawty. But anything is possible. Anything. Somebody who is not a woman, or even a man perhaps, may be getting called shawty right now, even as I speak."

Terrified, the advisor rifles through a cabinet of files.

I tell her to take it easy.

I ask what she's going to do about all of the time I lost essentially redoing my entire B.A. degree for no apparent reason. "You are an advisor, after all," I intone. "Advise me."

She dry-heaves.

"There are protocols," she says.

I wait for her to continue.

A toilet flushes in the next room.

"That's all you have to say about it? Do you even know what a protocol is?"

The sweep of my consequent aerostatic explanation is of course rooted in hard etymology, but the advisor doesn't want to hear about it.

My students were the same way.

They didn't want to hear about anything, no matter the context, or the subtexts, or the mere surface-appearance of the primary text or texts under scrutiny, let alone anything having to do with BwOs.

Students only want to pay their money and get their degree so that they can go do whatever else it is they want to do in the dining room or the bedroom or the bathroom or the basement of the House of Life.

Some students prefer to do what they do beyond House limits in the Pole Barn. But there is no escaping the House.

As Louis Althusser writes in "Ideology and Ideological State Apparatuses," a seminal piece of Marxist philosophy that I cited with habitual relish in my original dissertation, prompting my dissertation committee to refuse me the civility of crumpets and scones at our monthly get-togethers, an abnegation for which I have never forgiven my committee members: "What thus seems to take place outside ideology in reality takes place in ideology. What really takes place in ideology seems therefore to take place outside it." Later, Althusser adds: "Ideology has no outside. But at the same time, *it is nothing but the outside*." And what goes for ideology goes for *studentry*, a term I perhaps recklessly appropriate from Herrs Strunk & White in *The Elements of Style*, an entirely outdated grammar textbook written by a confused and to some extent incompetent English professor (Strunk) and the author of *Charlotte's Web* and *Stuart Little* (White). One enjoys the sound of the word *studentry*. And there is nothing more grotesque than *studentry*. Hence my deep interest in the grotesque. Exceptions belie the stereotype, of course, but exceptions are mere bric-à-brac; there are always too few of them to make a difference.

I get out my wine.

I ask where the wine glasses are.

The advisor pretends like she doesn't know what I'm talking about.

I pull a few sips from the bottle, cork it and put it away.

I get it out again and uncork it and put it on her desk and place the cork at the base of the bottle, leaning it against the glass so that it doesn't roll away. "Just in case," I remark.

Clearly the advisor can't or won't help me get back my time, money, and expended intellectual energy.

I say, "Who's a good dissertation advisor to pursue in my department?"

She asks me what department I'm in. I tell her.

She doesn't know anybody in that department.

I say, "I have a plan to get my dissertation done in a timely fashion. Many of my graduate students used to have difficulty with this. They completed their coursework and couldn't wrap their heads around the Final Stage. They were used to writing short essays, taking tests, and doing research, if they did any research at all. When they suddenly had to perform real research and produce a book-length manuscript, they faltered. And ultimately failed. Many of them never got past writing an introduction. In my case, I will print out my old dissertation in a new font and turn it in. This should take about five or ten minutes. I wrote it twenty years ago, but it's still relevant, and the prose is hip. My prose has always been hip."

My advisor says I can't do that.

I ask why.

She says I just can't do that.

I ask why again.

She doesn't know; people might not like it, though.

I ask why again.

She says I ask too many questions and questions often lead to hurt feelings.

I say, "Well just pretend I never brought it up. I won't plagiarize my old dissertation as far as you or anybody else knows. I'll write a new one from scratch."

"You can't take things back like that."

"They took my Ph.D. back."

"That's different."

I don't say anything.

The advisor says something.

I say, "Stand up and turn around so I can look at you. I have no idea what you look like from the opposite direction. You've been sitting there the whole time."

My quicksilver deflection works like a charm. Already she has forgotten what I said about turning in my old dissertation with a new font. And when she gets out of the chair, a new chapter unfolds.

41

"There's going to be a fire drill today."

"What?"

Timidly, tentatively, my roommate repeats himself.

"A fucking fire drill? Are you kidding me?"

"A fire drill," he says. "Nobody knows when it's going to happen. Everybody's betting on when it's going to happen. Some people are, like, I don't know . . . scared."

"Scared?"

He nods gravely. "Yeah. You know. Because of the sound. It's gonna be loud."

"Loud?"

He nods again.

"Are you fucking kidding me?"

He shakes his head.

I go talk to a Dean of something.

"What's this shit about a fuckin' fire drill?"

"Fire drill?" says the Dean. But he obviously knows there's going to be one.

"Fuck your fire drill. If I hear a fucking fire drill today I swear to god I'm gonna burn this goddamn hellhole to the ground! Dipshit!"

PRIMORDIAL

The Dean plays dumb for awhile longer. Eventually I get him to promise there won't be a fire drill.

When the fire alarm goes off, I'm sitting in ENG 801: Introduction to Graduate Studies.

Everybody screams.

"Stay calm!" exclaims the professor. "Stay in your seats, by God!"

Everybody stays in their seats.

The professor charges across the classroom towards the door. Students try to trip him and take out his legs. He's light of foot in spite of a terrific belly. Nobody even touches him.

The alarm is loud. My roommate was right. I'm scared.

The door won't open. The professor pounds on it and hollers for somebody in the hallway to open it.

Nobody opens it.

The students can't stand it any longer. They leap out of their chairs and make for the door.

They press against the professor, squeezing him into the cold wood.

His cheek presses against the glass window in the door, emboldening a popped blood vessel.

He moans.

The lights start blinking.

The floor starts shaking.

We slide across it in slowtime.

Unexpectedly, the professor collapses over a desk. I try to help him up. He shoos me away.

The fire alarm won't stop.

There might be a real fire somewhere.

Somebody says they see a fire out the window. "A real one," they emphasize.

We run to the window, trampling the professor. He begins to cough and choke. Long strands of plasma extend from his open mouth.

Next door a building is on fire. I don't even know what building it is even though I have used several of the toilets inside of it.

Venomous flames hiss and buckle in every exploded window and doorway.

There are people on the roof.

They're all on fire.

They screech and wail as they run back and forth like angry swarms of fireflies. Sometimes they crash into one another and fall off the roof.

The fire alarm keeps ringing even when the firemen show up, put out the fire, help the people, and go back to the fire station. Two days later it's still ringing.

Then it stops.

42

I get back from the wine store or the gym or gym class or somewhere or someplace and I catch my roommates doing the Macarena.

I've suspected this for a long time.

When I'm gone, they line-dance. I don't think they do much else.

They try to keep it to themselves because they think I'll shame and ridicule and symbolically castrate them.

When I interrupt them doing the Macarena, I can tell they're mad, because they really like that one, but anxiety trumps enjoyment, and they break out of formation and pretend to be inspecting the walls, and inspecting the ceiling, and inspecting their fingernails, and thumbing through textbooks that would otherwise remain permanently shut.

I say, "Were you just doing the Macarena?"

Their faces bunch in surprise and confusion. "Macarena?" says one of them, as if I'm speaking Spanish.

"Don't lie to me. I saw you doing the Macarena."

"What's the Macarena?" says another one.

Eyeballing him, I slowly pace across the room to the Victrola sitting atop the minifridge.

The title of the record has been crossed out with a thick black marker.

I adjust the fleur-de-lis, wind up the machine, maneuver the swing tube, and lower the needle onto the vinyl.

There's some static.

There's the music.

Then, finally, there's the chorus:

> *Dale a tu cuerpo alegria, Macarena.*
> *Que tu cuerpo es pa' darle alegria y cosa buena.*
> *Dale a tu cuerpo alegria, Macarena.*
> *Heeeeey Macarena. (Aaaaaiy!)*

I give the needle a flick and the music squelches off. I watch the record turn for awhile, then look over my shoulder and stink-eye the rabble. "That sounds like the fuckin' Macarena to me."

They all deny it.

Each of them has a different excuse as to why they weren't doing the Macarena.

One was studying.

One was playing a video game.

One was ordering a pizza.

One was daydreaming.

One recycles another one's excuse.

Another one recycles another one's excuse.

Etc.

I pretend to believe them before applying a chokehold of circular logic that broadsides their excuses and reveals their absurdity. This takes hours. I attend to each roommate in turn. By the time I'm finished with them, not only do they admit to line-dancing, they commence line-dancing, limbs swimming and synching like a cell of eels in an aquarium.

43

It's rush hour.

I accidentally cut off a pickup truck with jacked-up tires.

At the next stoplight the truck pulls next to me.

The driver rolls down the window.

He glares at me.

He says I drive a faggy car so I must be some kinda fag.

"Do Subarus denote homosexuality? This is a Forester, mind you. It's technically an SUV."

He swears at me. He tells me he's going to kill me.

"Well, if it helps, it's not my car. I 'borrowed' it from one of my roommates." I laugh.

He continues to threaten me. Then the light turns green. He rolls up his window. He flips me off.

We go.

I'm running low on gas. I stop to get some.

The pickup truck pulls into the gas station. The driver leaps out and marches toward me.

He's short.

He has a patchy beard.

He wears a plaid shirt and a trucker hat and all the rest of it.

I get out of the Subaru.

The driver reaches back a bloody stump.

I am a foot-and-a-half taller and 30 lbs. more muscular than him. At least.

He didn't realize it before. Everybody looks more or less the same behind the wheel of a car.

There's more talk of me being gay.

I take a step towards him.

He runs back to his truck.

As he retreats, I sort of yell at him in this resounding, preternatural death-voice. The modest subtext of my thesis: "You fucked with the wrong asshole, shithead."

The driver tries to get the truck going.

The engine hiccups. The starter won't catch.

There's an aluminum bat in the trunk of the Subaru.

I retrieve it.

I stride toward the truck.

The driver is getting antsy now. He peers at me in the rear view mirror. He hops up and down in his seat, stomping on the gas pedal.

I fall into a trot.

I lift the bat over my head.

I bring the bat down on the windshield of the truck, exploding it into glinting stardust.

The driver shrieks like an insect.

I hit the truck again with the bat. I hit the truck again with the bat. I hit the truck again with the bat. I hit the truck again with the bat. I hit the truck again with the bat. I hit the truck again with the bat. I hit the truck again with the bat. I hit the truck again with the bat. I hit the truck again with the bat. I hit the truck again with the bat. I hit the truck again with the bat. I hit the truck again with the bat. I hit the truck again with the bat. I hit the truck again with the bat. I hit the truck again with the bat. I hit the truck again with the bat.

I'm screaming like a pope, howling like a holy ghost. I hit the truck again with the bat.

The truck roars to life.

We go.

Violence begets violence. Ultraviolence is another matter. Hermeneutics of suspicion vary like words for snow in Eskaleut. And while violence in its pure form is certainly variable, it's not as volatile. This includes physical violence as much as the violence of Psyche and especially Rhetoric. Consider this climatic passage from Gilles Deleuze and Félix Guattari's *The War Machine*:

> The first theoretical element of importance is the fact that the war machine has many varied meanings, and this is *precisely because the war machine has an extremely variable relation to war itself.* The war machine is not uniformly defined, and comprises something other than increasing quantities of force. We have tried to define two poles of the war machine: *at one pole*, it takes war for its object, and forms a line of destruction prolongable to the limits of the universe. But in all of the shapes it assumes here— limited war, total war, worldwide organization—war represents not at all the supposed essence of the war machine, but only, whatever the machine's power

(*puissance*), either the set of conditions under which the States appropriate the machine, even going so far as to project it as the horizon of the world, or the dominant order of which the States themselves are no longer but parts. *The other pole* seemed to be the essence; it is when the war machine, with infinitely lower "quantities," has as its object not war, but the tracing of a creative line of flight, the composition of a smooth space and of the movement of people in that space. At this other pole, the machine does indeed encounter war, but as its supplementary or synthetic object, now directed against the State and against the worldwide axiomatic expressed by States.

Then, in the final sentence of the book, Deleuze & Guattari's thesis ignites like gunpowder: "War machines take shape against the apparatuses that appropriate the machine and make war their affair and their object: they bring connections to bear against the great conjunction of the apparatuses of capture and domination."

To adequately process this data, one requires an expansive knowledge of D&G's entire oeuvre, at which point the theoretical duo's enigmatic deployment of word-bombs becomes utterly ordinary, if not banal.

More compelling, perhaps, is a disembowelment of this material from the gutsack of everyday life. For instance, I get this text from my wife:

"Please go to the Dollar Store and pick up some butt-wipes for the baby."

But my phone has turned against me.

Also, as I remind my wife in an encrypted font: "I'm not home. I'm at school."

45

I say, "Did Mama Cass really choke to death on a hamburger?"

The grad student looks at the Professor. The Professor looks at the Dean. The Dean looks at another Dean. The other Dean looks at another Dean. That Dean looks at the Provost. The Provost looks at the President. The President looks at his mom.

His mom shrugs.

I say, "Well what good are you people? What good is any of this?" I gesticulate at the University.

46

My wife and I have an open relationship. Don't ask, don't tell.

I fall in love with my eschatology professor.

The swell of her bust cuts me deeper than the curve of her hips.

We make love beneath the moon.

Afterwards we lie naked on our backs in the grass and discuss the probability of the moon derailing from orbit and slamming into the earth like a great ball of scrimshaw, craters revealing themselves as open bear traps and *vagina dentata* etched into the ivory.

She ends her thoughts on the matter with a soft, awkward explosion from her lips. But not quite an explosion. More like a pop. And yet more violent than a pop.

"What lies between an explosion and a pop?" I ask her.

"Discourse," she whispers. "Rhetoric."

I take her breast in my hand and massage it. She tells me it doesn't feel good. I massage it differently. She says that feels worse.

I look at my hand.

The fingers, I realize.

The knuckles, I wonder.

My eschatology professor rolls on top of me. We set aside the pretense of language and gaze into each other's eyes. Our pupils have swallowed our irises. I can see the starlight reflecting off of my dark matter onto hers.

Later, we have sex in every public bathroom on campus, just to say we did it.

I do something she doesn't like. I say something she doesn't like. She tells me she doesn't like what I'm thinking.

She orders me to temper my metabolism.

I breathe in and out, in and out, in and out until I accomplish a fluid synesthesia, all of the extensions and vicissitudes of my sensorium called to stiff attention.

"I can hear your breathing," she remarks.

"Well I have to breathe. Don't I?"

"Not that way. You don't hear me breathing that way."

I release a cataleptic sigh. "I don't know what you want. I have tried to involve all of the senses. I have tried to account for the full breadth of human experience and potentially the experience of the moon. I am not the moon. I don't know what the moon thinks or what the moon desires or what the moon intends to do. You can't hold that against me."

She brushes a sandbug from her nipple. "I can hold anything against anyone. Your existential crisis is hardly my affair. Pull up your trousers and pretend you're a man. Better: pretend you're the moon. This is not a sitcom. We are all going to die and be forgotten someday."

There's nothing I can do to counter the argument. Once the certainty of oblivion is invoked, disavowal shotguns into plainclothesed entropy.

"That's my father."

The librarian points at something behind me. I glance over my shoulder.

There's a big poster. It occupies most of the wall.

On it is a rooster.

The rooster has a red mane and a red beard and cold eyes and a sharp beak and matted feathers and weird feet.

I eyeball the librarian. "Is that a photograph or an illustration? It looks real."

The librarian squints at the poster, makes a frog face, and shakes his head.

I say, "*Rooster* is slang for *male chicken*, you know. And slang for *rooster* is *cockerel*, but that's a Britishism. *Rooster*, on the other hand, is an Americanism. I don't see any balls on that cock either. Must be a *capon*. That's a slang term for *castrated rooster*, which is to say, *castrated cockerel*, by which I mean, *male chicken who has had his privates yanked off*."

The librarian taps his desk, tentatively, pensively, with a finger. "Are you calling my father a rooster?"

"Rooster?" I think about it. "Do you mean that rooster?"

Confused, the librarian has a nervous breakdown.

He tears off all of his clothes and runs through the stacks and up the stairs and down the stairs and he finds an ax somewhere and knocks over some bookcases and chops up some tables in a Quiet Area and then he gets tired and just kind of curls up and moans for awhile and the police come and leap upon him and put him in a straightjacket and drag him kicking and screaming out of the library.

On Monday, he punches in at 7:59 a.m.

I open the laptop.

I log onto a social network and find one of my professors. I friend him.

I wait.

A few seconds later the professor accepts my friendship.

I send the professor a message. It reads:

"What the fuck are you doing, asshole? Don't you think it's inappropriate for professors to be friends with their students like this? What the fuck? Pervert."

A few seconds later the professor unfriends me.

I close the laptop.

49

I mentioned something earlier about having only one active memory. That's not altogether true. Nothing ever is.

We are informed by history.

Subjective history, objective history.

Objectivity is a myth.

Here's another memory:

We were saving pennies to go to Disneyland. We put the pennies in a tall stained-glass container.

Years passed.

We didn't save enough pennies to get to Disneyland.

My stepfather did something to me and I refused to eat with him anymore.

Before dinnertime I would go into the kitchen and my mother would make me some food. I had to eat it as fast as I could before my step-father came home from work for the official family dinner.

Years passed.

One night I was late. I only had thirty seconds to eat. Mom tried to get things ready but there was no time.

My stepfather stormed into the kitchen. I slipped aside and went upstairs.

I waited.

I waited.

I waited.

After awhile I became deranged with hunger and I had to do something about it.

I went downstairs to the kitchen. There was my step-father counting all of the pennies and stacking them onto the counter. He stacked them as high as they would go until they fell over. He stacked them again until he could get a good read and the pile wouldn't fall over. Then he'd start a new pile.

I watched him from the wall corner.

He stacked and restacked and stacked and restacked and stacked and restacked the pennies until I fell asleep on the carpet.

Then he put the pennies away and went to bed.

50

I have lost track of what semester it is. I have lost track of how many semesters I have left. I have lost track of what my field of study is. I can't remember if I'm a student or a professor, a self or an other, a subject or an object, an Oversoul or the Underneath. Am I married? Do I own a house? Do I believe in God? When was my last meal? Have I ever hired a bodyguard? Do I care what people think of me? Do I write good books? What is the square root of the angle of my disposition? What happened to the tendons in my index finger? Do I go to my classes on a regular basis? Where is the men's room? Over there? Is that my 1966 Fender Bandmaster guitar amplifier? What has become of the guitar itself? Bass players worry me. I always have the feeling that they really want to be involved with a cello. But is it wrong to desire the cello above all else? Why must cortisol, epinephrine and norepinephrine pour into my bloodstream during moments of extreme panic? Can I have some more wine? Where did my copy of the latest issue of *The Journal of Bone and Joint Surgery* go? And the antelope? Is utopia possible or are we destined to endure the bogeys of nomad subjectivity and social Darwinism forever? Why do my armpits sweat all day long? Why wouldn't my students ever tell me when my fly was open? Why do I get good pumps during some workouts and bad pumps during other workouts? Can I have some more wine? Shawty! Does that professor like me? What's my grade point average? Is mankind proud of me? As a child, did I kill a bullfrog by hurling it against a brownstone with a makeshift trebuchet? Or did I merely hurl it into a pond? Given sufficient velocity, the frog explodes either way.

51

I give this guy my card. My "business" card.

There's only one word on it.

This word:

Miāo.

"That's onomatopoeia," I tell him. "But it's in a different language than the one we speak."

He blinks at me.

I say the word aloud, if only to encourage him, to assure him that the sum total of his fascia may not amount to the calibrated arrangement of his physiognomy. Therein lies my terminal modus operandi: to convince everybody, one social subject at a time, that they lack the fertility of tripe.

Nearby a Tesseract collapses into a morbid integer.

52

And so I thought to myself: . . . This *liebestod* is no mere subliminal excrescence. It is some queer manner of Faustian, brick-layered scatology. Do you think the emission of my selfhood into the commode is funny, or cute? I am on the threshold of transformation from overcoded schiz-flow to self-immolating becoming-tortoise, a process implicating certain transversals that will bind all of my vectors together and possibly jeopardize my admittedly destratified concept of molecular conformity. If only I had a beak; my dripping cathexis might have been subject to an entirely different manner of abjection. I remember—yes, I remember everything now, if only for a wilting and perilous moment—when I took the *agrégation*. I performed well on the examination despite my stepfather, who occupied the starboard flank of the classroom and heckled me, lobbing insults and scribbling fearsome genitals on the blackboard as a means of distraction. But nothing distracts me when I accomplish a certain quantum focus. I feel like I've done this before. I feel like I'll do this again. Once you engage a singularity you are doomed to fondle the ticklish parts of its shadow for eternity. The commiseration of meat. Chickenscratch.

The logic of sense. Damnation is a far cry from the blues. I have neglected to remain impartial to dogpoets. I mention dogpoets in all of my books. I don't know what they are.

53

I have a secret to tell somebody, anybody.

I go off campus to get my sushi.

The sushi that they serve in the cafeteria of the Student Union doesn't even qualify as sushi. It insults real sushi with its glib artificiality.

So I go to this place in the city.

Very covert.

None of the employees speak a word of English, but I can tell they like me. The inflection of their gazes indicates nothing to the contrary.

There's a problem.

Every time I eat my dish of sashimi salmon and tuna draped over sticky brown rice, I use more and more wasabi.

Every time.

At this rate, soon there will be only wasabi.

The fish, the rice, even the soy sauce and the garnish of pickled ginger—it will inevitably dwindle to an nth degree of meaning in the face of such Rampancy.

The laws of thermodynamics command it.

Zeno was not the idiot that the Eleans so desperately wanted him to be.

This doesn't stop me. I'm concerned. But I still need and want my sushi.

One day I go to get my sushi and the place is gone.

Not closed.

Gone.

There's a building, but it's not the same building.

There are no doors or windows.

It's really just a colossal, upended cinderblock. I wonder if anybody's trapped inside. The city looks different too.

I try to ignore it. All of it.

Depressed, I go back to campus.

I walk around for a couple of days. It gets dark and light and dark and light and the air is cool and warm and cool and warm and it always smells crisp and natural and earthy, like good incense.

At some point I realize the University has fallen apart.

Despite my situation, and despite faculty residences, I recall how the gothic beauty of the architecture used to invoke feelings of the Kantian sublime in my sensorium. How the seas of fog flowed beneath the stately, dark-bricked buildings and halls. How the cathedrals and the gymnasiums and the bibliotheques crouched beneath the heavens like autocratic Nephilim with garden-fresh breath. The elegant steeples. The cobbled turrets and their wayward belfries. Stone bridges ran between the tallest bluffs; they were at once medieval and futuristic. To walk among the architecture was to stand atop the Fell and gaze into the Tarn.

Now the University lies in ruins.

I don't remember when this happened. I don't remember hearing any buildings fall down.

My dorm is still intact. So are all of the administrative fortresses and sanctuaries and gazebos.

Everything else is rocks and dust, flotsam and jetsam, savannah and wind.

PRIMORDIAL

Professors roost on the debris teaching old books to brained students who lay comatose or dead in the gravel. I pass by one classwreck after another. The professors seem to have new springs in their pedagogical steps. Their eyes are sparkling and I can see their teeth and they're gesticulating with animation as they read aloud passages from assigned texts and pause to discharge canny hermeneutics that flow over the students like expanding rings of fire and ensure the certain fossilization of their bodies into the bones of the ragged earth.

It's a good dream. I'm sorry to see it dissolve into reality.

54

Existence is an illusion for the Blankness on the Other Side.

REVISION: Existence is an illusion for the Blankness that is the Otherside.

REVISION: Existence is nothing but a curtain that, yanked open, reveals the Empty Stage.

(NOTE: Stop capitalizing the first letters of select words in order to incite Big Signification in those words. It looks forced. And very dumb.)

REVISION: Existence is nothing but a big curtain that, yanked open by a fat man, reveals the organs that skim across the surface of the body electric like deranged waterbugs.

REVISION: One day deranged waterbugs will usurp the tyranny of bureaucratic echolalia.

REVISION: The harder you study, the dumber you get.

(NOTE: Cliché. And poorly written. All of it.)

REVISION: I can't get the theme song from that movie out of my head. Did I hear it recently somewhere or did my unconscious usher it onto the stage of my consciousness?

REVISION: I don't like my roommates. Not one of them. I miss my wife too. Not enough to call her. She'll just get mad. I'm mad enough for everybody.

REVISION: Madness is like life: it goes on and on and on and then somebody passes the baton.

(NOTE: No rhyming. No alliteration. No assonance.)

REVISION: There is only one Quasimodo. Everybody else is a crude imitation at best. And when the earth swallows the bell tower, all that remains are sonic memories and matte bronze skies.

REVISION: I don't want this for me. I don't want this for anybody. I've had too much coffee. I haven't had enough wine. One needs wine. One needs wine. One needs wine.

FINAL REVISION: Too much coffee, not enough wine.

55

I feel like I've lost something. Myself perhaps. Or somebody else. The rub is: Who is the Father dictating the angle of this adamantine repose?

The professor is explaining what we need to do for our upcoming essays. I don't understand what he means. I raise my hand. He calls on me.

I say, "So should we include a title page?"

The professor says, "No. As I pointed out about fifteen seconds ago, don't include a title page."

I say, "So no title page?"

The professor says, "No. No title page."

I say, "All right. No title page."

The professor says, "Yes. No title page."

I say, "I just want to be clear. You don't want a title page, right? Is that what you mean?"

The professor says, "That's right. No. I don't want a title page. That is precisely what I mean."

I say, "All right."

The professor says, "All right."

I say, "Why?"

The professor says, "What?"

I say, "Why? Why don't you want a title page? It introduces things, like."

The professor says, "Title pages are superfluous. A waste of space. And paper. Center your title at the top of the first page of your essay."

I say, "Center the title at the top of the first page of my essay. Right?"

The professor says, "Right. Center your title at the top of the first page of your essay."

I nod. Then I say, "Will we get points taken off if we include a title page? I'm only curious."

The professor looks at me.

I say, "Professor? Are you ok? You're just looking at me. Should I repeat my question?"

The professor says, "Again, no title pages. You shouldn't include a title page. There shouldn't be one. Don't include one. Don't include a title page. I don't want you to. Don't do it. No title page. Don't do it."

I say, "Don't do it."

The professor says, "Holy Christ."

I say, "But let's say we do it. Include a title page, I mean. Hypothetically, like. Will points be taken off?"

The professor says, "Whoever fights monsters—"

I interrupt, "Don't give me that Nietzsche shit. Everybody quotes that one anyway. Articulating that aphorism is more of an indication of a lack of erudition than an assertion of epistemological prowess. I'm talking about a title page."

The professor says, "Somber is human life, and as yet without meaning: a buffoon may be fateful to it."

I say, "That's a little better. But Nietzsche is really off-limits. Too commercial. If you want to sound smart, quote somebody like Feuerbach or Binswanger. Only real scholars know who they are. But I find it troubling that you can't come to grips with this title page debacle. I mean, for God's sake, who cares? It's not a big deal. I have ideas for fonts and so forth and you're really throwing a ratchet in my machinery here. I just want my essay to look as good as it can. A title page can make things look sharp, you know? Well." There's something else I want to say but I can't remember what it is.

The professor says, "The abyss."

I say, "That doesn't make any sense. Speak in complete sentences. That's a fragment."

The professor remains silent.

I say, "I assume your silence means a title page is ok. What else could your silence mean? Nothing."

The professor remains silent.

"Sir? Hey, you. You there. What the fuck are you doing? C'mon. Seriously? C'mon. No? Yes? Ok. All right. Yes or no. Don't answer that. It wasn't a question anyway. No. All right. Well. Well. Thank you, sir."

The professor remains silent.

I turn to the rest of the class and say, "Do you hear that? Title pages are ok. Go ahead and include one if you want to. Or don't. It's up to you. It's always been up to you. Nothing else matters but subjectivity and the unique arc of the human spirit."

56

I don't talk much about my fitness habits. I drink a lot of wine, but I hit the gym six days a week, sometimes twice a day, and while I will occasionally sip wine during cardio, particularly on stationary bikes and elliptical machines, for the most part I keep it clean. The point is, staying in good muscular and cardiovascular shape is part of my routine. The spectacle of my physique does not require the crutch of language.

57

On another, similar note:

I go to a college bar and they're shooting pornos all over the place.

In the restrooms.

On the dance floor.

Behind the bar.

I have more or less forgotten about pornos since they are shot everywhere, all the time, in every nook and cranny of college space and life. They have become as normative a fixture as the air I breathe.

Something about this particular spectacle piques my interest. It incites obsession, in fact, and I must drink large quantities of alcohol in order to exorcize the demons from my innerspace.

Drunk, I call my wife.

I try to tell her how I feel.

I slur my words and she gets mad and hangs up on me.

I call her back and tell her I'm sorry and hang up on her.

I call her one more time and assure her that I didn't mean to hang up on her. She didn't deserve that.

"How are the kids?"

"The kids?"

"How are the kids?"

"They're grown up."

"They're grown up?"

"They're grown up. They're not kids anymore."

I wobble back and forth. "What year is it?"

She tells me what year it is.

A student waiting for her scene brushes against me and leans onto the wall. She only has on a thong and her breasts and navel have been slathered with glitter. She looks at me through two puddles of mascara.

I look at her through blurred vision.

She moans perfunctorily.

I don't know if the moan is directed at me or if she's merely practicing her lines. I ask her.

She calls me a name and turns with a jerk.

I try to get her attention.

She's gone.

I remember that I'm on the phone. Nobody's there. I can't remember who I was talking to anyway.

58

Strobes of reality. Strophes of alterity.

I'm still drunk. It feels gud.

60

There's a raw fingerprint on the faux stainless steel, finger-print-proof kitchenette trashcan. Somebody must have left it there.

I confront my roommates.

"There's no fingerprint," responds one of them. "There can't be." He presses a fingertip against the siding and no fingerprint comes off.

"Don't get smart with me," I tell him.

I pass out.

My roommates put me on their shoulders, carry me to bed, and tuck me in.

I wake up with a hangover.

I go to the Union to get coffee and a bagel. No cream in the coffee. No cream cheese on the bagel.

All of the writers are dead.

They're strewn across the floors and the tables and the stairways and the railings and the embankments like wet papier-mâché mannequins. The pages of their manuscripts and their creative writing degrees tangle and snarl in the dust devils that rip across the floortiles and the grass and the bodies.

"Gesundheit."

A mortician takes me aside and asks if I will help clean up the mess.

"I don't know these people. Can't somebody else do it?"

The mortician insists there's nobody else.

I see people everywhere.

I say, "There's people everywhere. Seriously. Can't you ask somebody else? Him. Her. Her. Her. Her. Him. Her. Ask her."

The mortician doesn't want to. He likes the way I look. My brow, apparently, casts an attractive shadow onto the blank screen of my cheeks. "It's a shadow I can trust," explains the mortician.

"Fine. Fine. Fine. Fine. All right."

The dead writers smell terrible. Decomposition, let alone rigor, hasn't set in. This is how they smelled when they were alive. Slathering a mustache of mentholatum across my overlip doesn't help. I can still smell the writers. I worry that I'll never be able to get the smell off of me.

The mortician plays coach and directs me where to go. At first I defy him and demand that he disposes of some bodies too.

He won't do it. He's adamant. Almost arrogant.

On another day I may have let him have it, but I'm afraid of morticians, of their resolve, of their existential apathy, and I would do anything any mortician told me to do under any circumstances, although not without complaint. Like an unparented child, I never comply without the pretext of a complaint.

There are a lot of dead writers.

Students and faculty and staff and administrators and townies and other people that don't belong at the University stop and stare at me as I lift the bodies and hurl them into the mortician's jacked-up hearse.

There are dents all over the hearse. Especially on the hood. I assume they were produced by angry grievers who struck the vehicle with bats and bricks and sledgehammers as the mortician drove off with the corpses of their loved ones. I want to ask him if this is in fact the case.

I don't ask him.

After heaving about fifty writers into the trunk, I feel like I've caught something. I feel . . . dumb. And naïve. And invincibly self-important.

"I write because I'm weak!" I announce, slipping into character. I immediately regret it. Then I announce it again.

Before I can go on, the mortician kicks me in the knee and I fall over. Like a wrestler, he picks me up by the head, shakes me for about half a minute, then discards me. I do a maladroit somersault across the grass.

The audience cheers, claps.

I may or may not pass out. At no point do I lose the light, but there is a temporal gap.

Palsied, I stand and ask the mortician what happened.

He's gone.

And a new, much larger horde of writers have already overtaken the Union. Careworn manuscripts in one hand, creative writing degrees in the other, they stagger back and forth in search of fresh meat . . .

61

Nobody's looking at me anymore. It gives me time to think about things. This is the first thing I think: *I admire people who are not afraid to raise their naked limbs and reveal their untrimmed ditches.*

62

There is only realtime, slowtime, fasttime, outrétime and primaltime. If nothing else, I always try to account for each modality in the same protein-infused breath.

The snow comes down more horizontally than vertically and the wind sends ferocious ripples across the windowscreens on the porch, threatening to tear off the windowscreens and hurl them into the Loch. The corpses of Junebugs remain intact, the fingers of their insect limbs fused to the steel lattice. Nothing can evacuate them. Not even the heavy breaths of God.

I awake.

Headache. In the center of my forehead. The frontal lobe. It throbs.

Another memory swims to the delicate surface of my consciousness. The memory parts the headache like the Red Sea, relegating the pain to my temples.

I have a loose tooth. It's my first one.

My stepfather sees me wiggling the tooth with the tip of my tongue and drags me out to the Shed by the wrist, raking me across the gravel. I can feel the blood exit my knees despite my anxiety, my unbroken scream.

In the Shed, my stepfather stares hard into the middle distance as I nurse my wounds and plot my escape.

I hear insects.

My young brain lacks tactical prowess. I fail to accomplish even the vaguest gesture towards freedom.

The Shed is thin and tall and constricting. Not much room to move in here.

I can't see the roof. The walls rise into an elusive square of darkness.

The wall is full of instruments.

My stepfather selects an instrument.

"No," I say.

"I'm gonna get that tooth, boy. C'mere."

"No," I say.

"Gimme that tooth, boy. Gimme that old tooth in your head. I'm gonna get that old tooth."

"No," I say.

"You'll feel better. Man's gotta get his tooth yanked out sometimes. Makes a man a man."

"Stop it," I say.

"I'm not doing nothing."

"Stop it," I say.

"C'mere."

"No," I say.

He grabs me.

I scream.

He pries open my mouth.

I'm still screaming. Harder now.

He shoves the instrument into my mouth.

I choke.

He doesn't care.

The pain is excruciating. I might pass out.

I don't pass out.

I can feel the instrument.

It's breaking my teeth.

All of them.

My stepfather's grunting and shouting at me.

He wants the tooth.

I shouldn't have wiggled it.

I should never wiggle anything.

I miss the glad heyday of Critical Theory. I imagine the University ejaculated scholarly heterodox and dynamism from every gleaming orifice in that era.

But the tooth.

The tooth.

He's got it now, I think.

There's so much blood.

Red. Bright red. Hammer blood.

Not blood.

Blood is dark, like bile.

My blood.

My blood is bile.

Lipids beware.

You don't stand a chance.

The combustion chamber of my eventless gallbladder cannot possibly prepare you for the vagina dentata of my reckless duodenum.

My stepfather is pulling out all of my teeth.

Has pulled out all of my teeth.

I can't feel anything.

Numb.

I can't see anything.

Blind.

I can taste my bile.

And I can smell the Shed.

There's no way to describe it.

Analogies can't approach it.

Nothing smells like the Shed.

Nothing.

64

Mindful, I remember that it has been at least 48 hours since my last workout. Usually I go to the gym every day. Sometimes twice a day.

I confiscate one roommate's set of dumbbells and appropriate another roommate's Swiss ball. They hang their heads and I tell them to grow up.

I do a long set of dumbbell flyes on the Swiss ball. As I near the fiftieth rep, the Swiss ball explodes underneath me and the dumbbells fly out of my hands and one of them knocks somebody down and the other one bounces off of an unmade bed and crashes through a cobwebbed window.

The shriek of hate that emanates from my larynx is as inhuman as it is holy.

I deflate like an impaled zeppelin and cave into my soul.

All of my roommates rush to my aid. I stave them off with a pointed crowdstare. Eventually I am able to stand up and accomplish a few elementary stretches, assuaging my damaged vertebrae. This seems to make them happy.

65

It's getting late.

I'm getting old.

I don't recognize my image in the mirror anymore.

I try not to look at it.

I try to remember how many years I've been here, subtracting the years I was here the first time.

Decades have passed like microscopic gallstones.

Pornography has more or less eclipsed reality. I no longer recognize it. A genital is a genital is a genital.

To remove the Shoes. To walk backwards up the Slide.

I still have the same roommates. They used to differ considerably in age. Now everybody looks and acts the same, with the same drooping eyes, the same crumpled mouths, the same aching backs, the same overactive bladders, the same fits of insomnia and mania.

Most of my roommates have prostate cancer.

The ones that graduated had their degrees rescinded at the graduation ceremony. In the Gymnasium, the President of the University ordered them onstage and shook their hands with a smile and gave them their diplomas and after everybody got their diplomas they were all called back onstage one at a time and briefly castigated for breaking the rules and misbehaving and their diplomas were summarily confiscated by the President's henchmen and fed to a tremendous stone-age furnace.

Parents clapped.

Parents cried.

Then everybody returned to the dorm.

None of the faculty retire. They work until they die, often in the middle of lectures, barely able to articulate a coherent sentence or even stand up straight.

Administrators typically retire after two or three years, at which point they generally become fulltime Rotarians, spend more time on the golf course and the tennis court, and live forever.

This is not the case with the President, Provost, and several other kakistocrats.

They never retire.

They remain in office until somebody shoots them and claims their thrones.

I don't know what happens to the staff. They lack one of two vital ontological components: the power of capital or the awareness of intelligence. Hence nobody at the University cares about them.

I fear a certain dirge of unlearning.

I suspect a certain attenuation of spirit.

My screen of knowledge flickers like a black-and-white TV with bad reception. Sometimes I can only think in zigs, zags, and croaks of static.

And I can feel the tinfoil wrapped around my antennae.

It tastes like iodine.

I may be a Wagnerian *kaiju*.

I hear the music in the sky. Music is an important part of college life. Students identify themselves via the Song more than the Book or the Information or the Reality or the Bartleby. The Bartleby, above all, is what really matters.

He places the battery to the tongue, short-circuiting the taste buds.

The tongue shrivels in the mad gash.

He can't imagine the University ever existed without him. He can't imagine the University will go on existing after he passes away.

Likewise the University.

There is an epistemological intimacy between the two apparatuses. A meaningful connection.

To reboot.

To revert.

Hello! I exist.

Wind.

Cattails and sedges dance across the swamp as I crawl out of the mud and strike a pose behind the lectern.

I am naked and putrid and glorious.

Broken rhizomes slide down the trunk of my pink, ribbed musculature.

The members of the senate clap politely. I point at the moon, silencing them.

I try not to swallow the microphone when I speak into it like a pariah.

"We are all beleaguered by moments of doubt," I intone. "When in doubt, kill an animal. Not any animal. One of the creatures we have commercialized and eat on a daily basis. A cow. A chicken. A pig. Find one and get a machete. Gaze into its sad eyes for as long as you can. Then cut its goddamn head off. It might take more than a few blows. But you can do it. I repeat: you can do it. Shortly after the kill you will experience a marked withdrawal of the doubt in question. It may or may not return. The good news is that, if it does return—now you know what to do."

Something happens here.

And here. Something monstrously pornographic in both instances. *Quippe.*

For the record, paganism suits me. The Ovidian gods. Why shouldn't there be a plurality of sex-crazed deities with volcanic insecurities and apocalyptic mean-ons?

I don't miss my students.

68

I call my wife.

"You're right in front of me," she says.

I hang up the phone. "I'm sorry," I say.

"I know," she says.

"I'll make it up to you," I say.

"I know," she says.

"How are the girls?" I ask.

She smiles. "They're good. They're playing in the dark."

I don't smile. "That's good." I don't smile again. I haven't smiled in years. "Do you think they remember me?"

My wife trashes the kitchen. "Maybe. Probably. You're their father. You're the rock," she explains.

I nod. "Right. Right. Right. Right. I understand. That makes sense. Right. Right. Right. Right. Right. Right. Right," I say.

I love my wife and kids.

I really do.

These people, technically speaking, are all that matter.

My fixations, my traumas, my anxieties, my badnesses, my fetishes, my appetites, my significations, my out-of-the-corner-of-the-mouthisms, my deployments, my aggressions, my capers, my idolatries, my indictments, my litigations, my verdicts, my peripeteias, my mournings, my emissions, my gesticulations, my dominations, my litterbuggings, my panderings, my scourgings, my reapings, my hate-mongerings, my bench-pressings and my binge-drinkings—all of these things, individually and collectively, are neither here nor there.

I think I forgot to study for that midterm exam I got to take tomorrow. I'll have to pull an All Nighter.

I tell my roommates to get out. They don't want to go but they know they don't have a choice.

I lock the door behind them.

Around 3 a.m. the dead begin to speak to me.

Black ghosts have confiscated the white noise.

I examine the Victrola to make sure that it's working.

It is.

I perceive the voices of deceased autocrats contacting me from the Underworld. Their clipped accents belie their opaque intentionality.

I get the sense that the voices will never go away.

I turn off the Victrola.

They go away.

71

A fight breaks out during the midterm. I start it.

72

Sushi "goes extinct."

You can't get it anymore.

Not on campus, not off campus.

And when I ask somebody about sushi, anybody, they look at me funny, uncertain of the word's meaning.

It's gone.

When something close to you dies, you change forever.

There is no sushi.

Again: there is no sushi.

One more time . . .

I can't get over the "extinction of sushi."

I think about it every day.

I carry the Lack with me wherever I go.

I feel guilty, as if I were responsible.

As if, somehow, I "killed sushi."

All of the sushi.

This is a simple enough delusion, but I am powerless to rise above it, to disavow it, to banish it from the cockpit of my subjectivity.

My awareness that the delusion in question is a real delusion—i.e., that the delusion exists, thus distorting my perceptive faculties—is of no consequence. It never is. And this is my distinguishing characteristic.

And this, above all, is why I am just like everybody else.

73

One of my roommates dies.

It's his ninety-third birthday.

We make him a cake and he gets so excited he begins to hyperventilate and he can't calm down.

We watch him.

His skin turns purple. His veins inflate. His cheeks puff out. He grips fistfuls of air. He makes a sound like a toad trying to play a flute. He makes another sound like an imploding brick.

Eventually he falls sideways onto a chair, smashing it.

Nobody knows CPR.

That makes my eldest roommate eighty-nine now. I tell him he's in charge and sort of laugh until my stomach hurts. Then I ask if he likes me. I ask all of my roommates if they like me.

"I just want to be liked," I admit.

Anticlimax is like Malbec. Varietal and robust. Full and dry.

75

I strike one of my professors.

He is very old.

Elderly.

And he's lying in bed.

A hospital bed.

I'm in the Infirmary.

It might be the Morgue.

It's the Morgue.

And the professor is dead.

He says, "Please. Please."

The mortician appears. He remembers me, complimenting the shadows that "sleep on my cheeks." They remind him of the dark side of the moon.

I say something about how my professor is dead and said please twice and the mortician replies, "Yes. But the glaucoma, you see."

I look down into my professor's frozen-open eyes.

There are no pupils, no irises. Only milky films that seem to glow in the purple darklights of the Morgue.

Saddened, I turn to the mortician. "All this death. All these empty shells. How do you do it?"

"Everybody dies. Can you give me a hand?"

He wants me to carry the body across the room and deposit it in what looks like a fish tank or some kind of incubation chamber that will, according to the mortician, "suck the residual life out of it."

Objecting, I try to run away.

The mortician talks me into Stasis.

Then he talks me into doing what he wants.

I only get about halfway across the room, the dead professor slung over a shoulder, before my back gives out and I collapse.

I groan.

"You are very old," utters the mortician, trying to help me up. "Elderly, one might say."

I shoo him away and push the cadaver off of me and get up myself, clutching my lower back.

This takes awhile.

The mortician encourages me to buy a coffin. "It's never too early to plan for The End."

Once I'm on my feet he pushes me into another room where there are several varieties of coffins for sale.

He drags me around by the elbow and tells me about the exteriors and the interiors and the discounts and the pros and cons of this coffin versus that coffin.

I want to resist.

I hurt too much to stop the mortician. I don't want to make him mad either.

Nonetheless I inform the mortician that there's no way in hell I'm buying a coffin.

The mortician is tenacious. He wants a down payment.

I tell him no.

The mortician keeps after me. He won't let up.

Neither will I.

At some point I lie down and close my eyes.

76

I get a letter and it says my parents are dead. Mother's cause of death: old age. Father's cause of death: grief.

No signature. No return address.

It has been years since I've seen my parents.

Their last visit was over a decade ago.

I barely remember what they look like, and I don't own any photographs, not of them, not of anybody, or anything.

The ability of the photograph to freeze time is something I have always deeply resented. Frozen time is no time at all.

I call my wife to break the news but the line has been disconnected and I can't be sure that I even own a phone anymore. I'm not sure I even know what a phone is.

When I reach behind myself and bend over, my arthritis flares and kicks like an impaled bull.

Grooming my body hair has become too much work.

I let the hair grow out.

The moment I make the decision, the hair bristles . . . and stops growing.

Two weeks later my thighs are smooth as ice, white as ivory. I touch them and the feeling is gone.

78

Weary, I sleep for at least a fortnight.

A monkey attacks the University as I lay unconscious.

It is not a big monkey but it is a powerful monkey and a purposeful monkey and the administrators don't know what to do. They're scared. And yet everybody more or less likes monkeys. Even the evil, destructive ones.

Prudence is required.

Faculty and staff don't have an opinion on the matter. They left the University long ago. Or died.

Nobody here notices when people die.

Meanwhile the monkey wreaks unmitigated havoc. How are we to negotiate its hambone antics?

Right now the monkey is tearing across campus throwing bricks through all of the windows that have not yet been shattered by drunken students, deranged faculty, choleric staff and bored vandals.

"That's no bonobo," remarks the President, and takes refuge in a bomb shelter . . .

. . . inevitable postapocalyptic dreamscape clinched by the flexed biceps of Logic. When reality gets hairy, the best medicine is Hard Science.

Hard Math in particular.

Consider Euclidean geometry, namely the Pythagorean theorem—my theorem of choice:

$$a^2 + b^2 = c^2$$

But even the monkey can perceive the holes in this pre-Socratic-addled configuration. Euler's Identity presents a greater challenge:

$$e^{i\pi} + 1 = 0$$

See how the monkey swings from the bowed undercarriage of Pure Energy to the collapse of numeric stability and the beginning of rawhide code . . .

The question remains as to what is the most popular square root.

This ushers us into the realm of cubic functions.

My typewriter lacks the capacity to format seven-story equations on a mere sheet of paper.

I will need a CAD processor.

Does anybody have a CAD processor I can borrow?

Does anybody know what a CAD processor is?

Anybody? Anybody?

In any case the monkey has confiscated my typewriter and smashed it over the head of a prominent trustee, one who has donated upwards of ten million dollars to the University in the last five years alone. Needless to say the trustee is dismayed and rallies with a crowbar, but the monkey has anticipated a rejoinder and fled to the bell tower, where it attempts to dismantle the primary carillon and hollow out the upper shaft.

Meanwhile, in my dreams, I am flying above a catacomb, and I am committing arson upon the haunted house of my psyche, and I am contemplating an equation related to dark energy, a (non)substance whose ontology flirts with that of the Lacanian Real.

Generally the equation makes sense.

I understand at least three-fourths of it at first glance and I can envision certain integers and combinations of integers flowing down the fiberoptic waveguides of its machinery. Integers stall periodically when they pass through the sphincter of Hubble's constant, and the final, bottommost plateau is deceptively conspicuous in terms of its moral stance. A bird's eye view reveals that the equation is a hoax, a kind of anaphoric pop melody that tries to be smarter that the summation of the dumb molecules that comprise its bawling physique.

The monkey excitedly concurs . . . and then dies.

It loses its footing and falls twenty stories down the shaft of the bell tower into the cellar.

One wonders if the primate committed suicide or if its demise was a bona fide accident.

Unexpectedly aggrieved (yet admittedly relieved), the administrators go downstairs, gather in a wide circle around the corpse, and wait for somebody to say something nice, sipping spoiled wine from makeshift decanters.

79

This one's for the ones who need Help . . .

I walk down a hallway. I walk down a hallway. I walk down a hallway. I walk down a hallway. I walk down a hallway. I walk down a hallway. I walk down a hallway. I walk down a hallway. I walk down another hallway. I walk down a hallway. I walk down a hallway.

I walk down a hallway.

I walk down a few more hallways. There's another hallway that I walk down. One more.

One more.

I keep going.

I walk down a hallway.

I come to another hallway and walk down it.

Then another hallway.

Then another one.

Then another one. Then another one. Then another one. Then another one.

Then another hallway.

Another.

Another.

Another.

Another.

Another.

Another.

Another hallway.

I turn a corner and bump into a priest.

He drops all of his scriptures and stares hatefully at me.

"Sorry."

Now I amble down a hallway.

I'm ambling now. Before I was just walking.

It makes a difference. Ambling and walking are like day and night in some cultures.

I amble down a hallway.

I amble down another hallway.

Then another hallway.

Then another one.

Ambling now.

Ambling.

Ambling.

Ambling.

Ambling.

Ambling.

Ambling.

I pause. I don't know why.

I smell the air.

I make a face.

I start ambling down a hallway again.

I'm ambling again.

Ambling.

Ambling.

Ambling down a hallway.

Ambling.

Ambling.

Ambling.

Ambling.

Ambling.

Ambling.

Narrative as Blot. Lived experience as Blot. Primordial soup and End as Blot.

That's all of it.

Ambling down a hallway . . . Repetition is just as good as karma. Once you embrace it, once you ingest it—you're bound to wallow in it.

89

It is not difficult to be a cutout, a cutup, or a cutthroat. To be authentically labyrinthine is even easier. Such conditions are in fact effortless, joyous . . . until you become aware of them. Then the curtains raise.

The best truths are the simplest idiocies.

81

Somebody drives by the front gate of the University in a minivan. They're going fast.

The back doors of the minivan butterfly open and somebody else throws out a body.

The minivan speeds away.

The body rolls across the grass like an unmanned ventriloquist doll.

I happen to be kneeling there. A long time ago my geology professor told me to find some good rocks. "The best rocks," he insisted, "are near the front gate, hidden in the grass."

I've been looking ever since.

The body has been wrapped in cellophane.

I pace across the grass and flip it over and tear open the cellophane so I can see the head.

It reminds me of the head of my dissertation advisor.

It's thin and gray and haunted by corpuscles.

So unlike my dissertation.

My dissertation was dense and vibrant and invigorated by Desire. I miss it more than I miss my own youth and the feeling of sand between my toes.

I cover the head.
I don't bury the body.
And when the mortician shows up, I'm gone.

82

I'm throwing grenades into a lake.

I don't know where I got the grenades and I don't know what lake this is.

It doesn't look familiar.

The water is gray.

I'm in a boat.

A pontoon boat.

Occasionally sunlight glints off of the shiny metal frame and stabs me in the eye.

I might be stranded.

It doesn't worry me.

After I pull their clips, I put the grenades to my ear and shake them, softly, like a rattle, to see if I can hear them tic. Then I cast them into the water.

There's a pause.

Then a detonation—a muffled, rumbling blast that, after another pause, spits a morass of dead fish to the surface.

Perch, mostly.

Some white bass and sheepshead.

Sometimes I stop to drink wine.

I'm almost out of wine.

I wish it would rain. The sound of rain on water is the stuff of warm dreams.

When the wine is gone, I'll just keep feeding grenades into the lake, one by one, until something happens.

Only two things can happen.

One: I kill all of the fish.

Two: I run out of grenades.

I'm out of grenades.

All of the fish are dead.

In the distance, the University lays on the shore like an evacuated whale . . .

Berserk paillasse of violence.

84

Do you ever get the feeling that your molecules are dirty? My molecules feel like Biblical whores.

Liebestod.

Hello! I exist.

Burn in hell.

I am not afraid of poi.

I invented plaster, however.

Reboot. Revert.

Hydrogen, helium, and a pinch of lithium.

Ich bin nicht ein glücklicher Mann.

I call to the long quasars in the rafters, in the hay.

I do not believe in superpowers. And yet I feel alive.

And when I forget to put on underwear, it feels gud.

Sadly, I am correct.

Datum.

The sum of human desire, consequence, suffering and madness can be attributed to two seminal factors: audacity and fear.

And now I will take a bath. In a tub.

There is no tub.

I am not the ghost of my former self.

I have never eaten a jelly donut. I never will.

Please check out my website. It's full of porn and insight and darkness.

Everybody loves it.

I hate your guts.

How old am I?

I don't want to die.

Maybe I'll be the first one to live forever.

Shawty doesn't even know how much I think about her.

Who doesn't clean their garbage cans and their sponges and their broomheads on occasion?

Methods of Keeping Things Clean must be kept clean too. Otherwise: chaos.

Who is casting that shadow on her lunar anus?

Adjust the lighting please.

Everybody take a step back please.

Thank you.

My stepfather and my real father are as much the same person as they are themselves and entirely different entities.

There is no (step)father.

This is a good life.

I like reading about the moon.

Everything is black and white and nothing really happens and the landscape is just beautiful and I can jump, like, a hundred feet into the air.

I'm alone too.

I used to despise loneliness but I've become exceedingly addicted to it.

I think when you die you get to go to the moon.

Everybody gets to go to the moon.

Their own moon.

As I prepare to leap over a yawning impact crater, I lose my footing.

Discombobulation.

I crawl across the tundra until I hit a wall. Ragged solar winds peel the skin from my face.

I'm ok.

I consider the low albedo, the bi-hemispherical reflectance, the epoxies that combust on the stage of mourning.

I climb a ladder and jackknife off of the high-dive into the cool waters of the Void, producing tall eruptions of aftershock and dark matter and angel paste that burn holes in the ceiling of reality.

Soup. Surf. Eukaryote.

Monkey.

Shawty.

The sun swallows the sky.

The moon swallows the sun.

God swallows the moon.

The Universe looks awry.

85

Like tubs, like sushi—there is no University.

This is as it should be.

Tabula rasa.

I've said it before.

Remember?

Streets paved with glands, architectures paved with ether, intellects and ideologies evaporating into the veiled interstices of time and space. All that remains are the echoes of penetration, of flesh on flesh, a moist pop, performative gazes and eerie cottonmouths opening onto the wasteland.

I can't tell if the libraries have been blown up or eviscerated like obese criminals.

The books are harder to look at than the bodies.

Memories produce turbulence in my lines of flight.

I must grip the armrests for support.

Vespers.

Ambience.

Over there is an elevator.

Where did it come from?

What's an elevator doing at the University? There are only stairs at the University.

I have never seen an elevator outside the confines of its shaft. It looks naked.

The elevator is broken.

The elevator is on its back.

In the dead cornfield.

In the dry scales.

I circle the wreckage and gauge its semantic impact, its karmic potential. Then I pry open the doors with a crowbar and climb inside.

I take off my t-shirt.

I take off my sweatpants and my underwear.

I press a cheek against the walls of the mirrored chamber.

The mirrors are broken and the shards are sharp. They cut into my skin like unspeakable clichés.

I can feel the blood rolling down my face.

It feels gud.

Outside there are birds that don't tweet and there are stars that don't glint and the air doesn't smell like anything.

And once again: this is as it should be.

This history, this reality, this future . . . and dreams of wasabi slouching across the enormity of my tongue.

D. HARLAN WILSON is an American novelist, short story writer, literary critic, editor, historian, and English prof. Visit him online at **DHarlanWilson.com** and **TheKyotoMan.com**.